ON THE CALCULATION
OF VOLUME

First published in 2024
by Faber & Faber Ltd
The Bindery, 51 Hatton Garden
London ECIN 8HN

First published in Danish in 2020 under the title
Om udregning af rumfang I by Pelagraf, Denmark

Typeset by Faber & Faber Ltd
Printed in the UK by CPI Group (UK) Ltd, Croydon CRO 4YY

*This is a work of fiction. All of the characters, organisations
and events portrayed in this novel are either products of the author's
imagination or are used fictitiously*

A CIP record for this book
is available from the British Library

ISBN 978–0–571–38337–5

2 4 6 8 10 9 7 5 3

ON THE CALCULATION OF VOLUME

BOOK I

SOLVEJ BALLE

*Translated from the Danish by
Barbara J. Haveland*

faber

121

There is someone in the house. Heard as he moves around the room upstairs. When he gets out of bed or when he goes down the stairs and into the kitchen. There's the gush of water through the pipes when he fills a kettle. The sound of metal on metal when he sets the kettle on the stove and the very faint click when he turns on the gas. Then there's a pause until the water comes to the boil. There's the rustle of tea leaves and paper as first one, then another spoonful of tea leaves is taken from a paper bag and poured into the teapot, then the sound of water being poured over the tea leaves, but such sounds can only be heard in the kitchen. I can hear the fridge being opened, because the door bumps against a corner of the worktop. Then there's another pause, while the tea steeps and in a moment I'll hear the chink of a cup and saucer being taken from the cupboard. I don't hear the sound of the tea being poured into the cup, but I can hear footsteps moving from the kitchen to the living room as he carries the cup of tea through the house. His name is Thomas Selter. The house is a two-storey stone cottage on the outskirts of the town of Clairon-sous-Bois in northern France. No one enters the back room overlooking the garden and a woodpile.

I

It is the eighteenth of November. I have got used to that thought. I have got used to the sounds, to the grey morning light and to the rain that will soon start to fall in the garden. I have got used to footsteps on the floor and doors being opened and closed. I can hear Thomas going from the living room to the kitchen and putting the cup down on the worktop and before long I hear him in the hall. I hear him take his coat from its peg and I hear him drop his umbrella on the floor and pick it up.

Once Thomas has gone out into the November rain there is silence in the house. Broken only by my own sounds and the soft patter of rain outside. There is the scratch of pencil on paper and the scrape of the chair on the floor when I push it back and get up from the table. There are the sounds of my footsteps as I cross the room and the very slight creak of the door handle when I open the door into the hall.

While Thomas is out I usually wander around the house. I go to the toilet, get water from the kitchen, but I soon go back to the room. I close the door and sit down on the bed or the chair in the corner, so I won't be seen from the garden path if anyone should look in.

When Thomas returns carrying two thin plastic bags the sounds start up again. The key in the door and shoes being wiped on the mat. The crinkle of the plastic bags when he sets down his shopping. The sound of the rolled umbrella, which he lays on the chair in the hall, and a moment later that of his coat being hung on the rack by the door. I hear the repeated crinkle of plastic as he places his carrier bags on the worktop and puts things away. He puts cheese in the fridge, pops two tins of tomatoes into a cupboard and leaves a bar of chocolate on the worktop. When the bags are empty he crumples them up and stows them in the cupboard under the sink. Then he closes the door and leaves them to carry on crinkling in there.

During the day I hear him in the office upstairs. I hear a swivel chair rolling across the floor and the printer churning out labels and letters. I hear footsteps on the stairs and the gentle thud on the floorboards as Thomas sets down parcels and letters in the hall. I hear him in the kitchen and the living room. I hear the sound of a hand or a sleeve brushing the wall as he goes back upstairs, I hear him in the bathroom and I hear a sound from the toilet that can only be made by a man peeing upright.

Presently I hear him on the stairs and in the hall again, then he goes into the living room and sits down in an armchair by the window facing the road. And there he waits, reading and watching the November rain.

He is waiting for me. My name is Tara Selter. I am sitting in the back room overlooking the garden and a woodpile. It is the eighteenth of November. Every night when I lie down to sleep in the bed in the guest room it is the eighteenth of November and every morning, when I wake up, it is the eighteenth of November. I no longer expect to wake up to the nineteenth of November and I no longer remember the seventeenth of November as if it were yesterday.

I open the window and throw out some bread for the birds that will soon be gathering in the garden. They show up when there is a break in the rain. First the blackbirds, who peck at the last apples on the apple tree or the bread I've thrown out, and then a lone robin. Moments later a long-tailed tit flies down, closely followed by some great tits who are promptly seen off by the blackbirds. Shortly afterwards the rain comes on again. The blackbirds carry on feeding for a little while longer, but when the rain gets heavier they fly off to take shelter in the hedge.

Thomas has lit a fire in the living room. He has brought in wood from the garden shed and I soon start to feel the house growing warmer. I heard the sounds from the hall and the living room, but now that Thomas is sitting reading, all I can hear is my pencil on the paper, a whisper, soon eclipsed by the sound of the rain.

I have counted the days and if my calculations are correct today is the eighteenth of November # 121. I keep track of the days. I keep track of the sounds in the house. When it is quiet I do nothing. I lie down and rest on the bed or I read a book, but I make no sound. Or hardly any. I breathe. I get up and tiptoe about the room. The sounds carry me around. I sit on the bed or gently pull the chair out from the table by the window.

In the middle of the afternoon Thomas puts on some music in the living room. First I hear him in the hall and the kitchen. I hear him putting a kettle on the gas ring, hear his footsteps on the floor as he goes back through to the living room and puts on the music. Then I know it will soon clear up. The clouds will pass and there will be a glimmer of sunshine.

I usually get ready to go out as soon as the music starts. I get up and put on my coat and my boots. I stand by the door for a few moments until the music is so loud that I can leave the house without being heard, the strains issuing from the living room masking the sound of doors being opened, of footsteps on the floor and doors being closed.

I leave the house by the garden door. I slip my bag over my shoulder, softly open the guest-room door, step into the hall and close it behind me. On the floor are three medium-sized envelopes and four brown cardboard parcels with our name on them: T. & T. Selter. That's us. We deal in antiquarian books, specialising in illustrated works from the eighteenth century. We buy the books at auction, from private collectors or other booksellers and then sell them on, sending them off in brown parcels bearing our name. I slip silently past the parcels on the floor, open the door and step outside. I don't need an umbrella. It is still raining slightly, but it won't be long before it stops completely. I don't take the garden path leading up to the gate, instead I turn left and go around the side of the house, past the shed and on down to a corner of the garden that can't be seen from the house. I pass a plot of leeks and two rows of Swiss chard and come to a gap in the fence which brings me out onto the road. I glance back briefly. I see a thin trail of smoke coiling up from the chimney, hear the very faint sound of music, but I hurry on. A few steps further and I can hear neither music nor rain because the rain has stopped, the music has been left behind me and the only sounds are my footsteps on the pavement, the rumble of a few cars and the distant voices of children at a school some streets away.

Not long afterwards, when Thomas sees that the rain has stopped, he turns off the music. He puts on his coat and picks up the pile of letters and parcels from the hall floor. He leaves the house at 15.24. Carrying letters and parcels. T. & T. Selter. That's us. But time has come between us. We walk along the narrow roads into town or back to the house. We are outside, we walk around in a break in the rain, but we do not take the same roads. He does not expect to meet me along the way, nor will he. I know another route and by the time he returns to the house I am back in the room looking out onto the garden.

If there is anything I need I buy it in a small supermarket a couple of streets over. I allow plenty of time and usually take a roundabout way home. I come through the gate and up the garden path to the back door and let myself in. The house is quiet. Thomas is out and it is no longer raining. He is on his way into town and by the time he has dropped off his parcels the sun will have broken through. He will take a walk through the woods and down to the river and won't return until late in the afternoon after the rain has started again, because there is no one waiting for him in the house and there is nothing he has to do.

Usually, when I return I leave my shopping in the guest room. I hang my coat over the back of the chair, I take off my boots and go through to the kitchen. There's a cup next to the sink and the kettle on the stove is still slightly warm. I can follow Thomas's tracks through the house. I go upstairs and into the office. There are piles of books on the desk and a scattering of papers. There are books on the shelves and in boxes on the floor. One of the boxes is open because Thomas has been searching through it for something and hasn't closed it again. In the bedroom next door to the office it looks as though someone has just got up, but only one side of the bed has been slept on.

I have an hour and half in the house before Thomas gets back. I have time to have a bath or wash some clothes in the sink, I have time to take a book from the shelf and sit down with it in one of the armchairs by the window.

If I spend the time in the living room I usually listen to music or read until it starts to get dark, but today I am staying in here, in the room overlooking the garden and a woodpile. I heard Thomas take his coat off the peg and I heard him leave the house. I opened the door into the hall, the packages are gone from the floor and now I am sitting at the table by the window. It is the eighteenth of November. I am becoming used to that thought.

On the morning of the seventeenth of November I said goodbye to Thomas at the door of the house. The time was quarter to eight, the taxi was waiting outside and I caught the 8.17 train from Clairon-sous-Bois. I was going to Bordeaux for the annual auction of illustrated works from the eighteenth century. The sky was grey, there was moisture in the air, but it didn't come to rain.

From Clairon station I travelled to Lille-Flandres, switched to Lille-Europe and went from there to Paris, where I changed trains for Bordeaux. I got to the station in Bordeaux just before two o'clock and after a moment's confusion due to roadworks outside the station, with lots of barriers, signs and closed footpaths, I found my way to the exhibition centre where the auction was to be held, arriving there a few minutes later. I registered and was given a programme and a badge that read '7ème Salon Lumières', followed by my name, and below that our company name, T. & T. Selter.

I was in good time for the main auction of illustrated books, which was due to start at three o'clock. A couple of auctions had already been held and I could see from the programme that again this year there would be talks and panel discussions, but none that I was planning to attend.

Once inside I faltered for a moment, again slightly disoriented by a scene that spoke of a conference in progress, all closed doors and abandoned coffee cups, until I spotted the signs and arrows pointing to the auction room and the adjoining exhibition hall where scores of antiquarian booksellers had, as always, set up their stands displaying books and scientific illustrations. I had a fairly good idea of which books I wanted to bid for in the auction and once I had taken a look at the most important of these I did a round of the exhibition hall. I said hello to some booksellers I knew from before and then, at a few minutes to three, I took my seat in the auction room, which soon began to fill up with people streaming out of the conference rooms.

I managed to buy twelve works at the auction. Five for which we had already had requests and seven others for which I thought we could get decent prices. We deal mainly in moderately priced books and sell to a mixed bunch of collectors, most of them in Europe, although we do also have a few customers in other parts of the world. As a rule I am the one who travels to auctions and visits antiquarian bookshops while Thomas takes care of cataloguing and shipping.

To begin with we did everything together, but we have gradually split the responsibilities between us. I'm not sure why it fell to me to do the travelling. Maybe because I don't mind travelling so much and maybe because I very quickly developed a certain instinct for the books, a feel for the paper, an eye for the quality of the printing, for a well-crafted binding. I don't know what it is, but it's almost physical, like an inchworm testing whether a leaf is worth creeping across, or a bird listening to the movements of insects in the bark of a tree. It might be a detail: the sound when you flick through the pages, the feel of the lettering, the depth of the imprint, the saturation of the colours in an illustration, the precision of the details in a plate, the colouring of the edges, I don't know what it is that seals it for me, because even though I generally know which works I'm interested in, usually I'm not absolutely sure whether I want to buy a book until I have it in my hand.

After the auction I went back to the exhibition hall, paid for some books I had had put aside and found another six works that I had been looking for, as well as a few I hadn't known about. I usually arrange for the heaviest and most valuable books to be sent straight to Clairon-sous-Bois, but I often take a few of my purchases away with me in my bag: on this occasion a pocket encyclopedia of bird calls arranged by note, new to me; a second edition of Harcard's book on the anatomy of animals and a fine copy of Boisot's renowned book on spiders, *Atlas des Araignées*, which one of our regular customers wished to give as a present to a friend and which we had therefore promised to look out for.

Late in the afternoon on the seventeenth of November I boarded the train to Paris and arrived late that evening at the Hôtel du Lison, where we usually stay when we're in town. The Hôtel du Lison sits on the corner of the rue Almageste, where several of the antiquarian booksellers with whom we deal have their shops and where our good friend Philip Maurel has his antique coin shop. My plan for the next two days, apart from buying books for our business and seeing Philip, was to visit the research library, Bibliothèque 18, in Clichy where I had an appointment on the nineteenth with a librarian by the name of Nami Charet, who had written an article on some hitherto overlooked variations on eighteenth-century printing techniques. Her discovery of certain changes to engravers' tools and working methods had made it possible to date illustrations from the end of that period with great accuracy, thereby shedding light on discrepancies between their genesis and the year of publication.

Once at the hotel I called Thomas. It wasn't a long conversation. I told him about the day's finds and asked him if he had any titles to add to my list for the next day. He had come up with a couple of works which he thought would be worth looking for and he had also just arranged with two of our fellow dealers in the rue Renart, a side street off the rue Almageste, to have a couple of books set aside. He asked me to examine them, and to buy them if they were in decent condition. I added these titles to my list and promised to take a look at them. I think we chatted a little more about the auction and a bit about the November weather before we said our goodnights and hung up.

We try to avoid long phone calls when we're apart. Not only because otherwise we would only end up having long, detailed dialogues on the condition of the books, publication years, the illustrations and the pricing but also because such conversations seem to increase the distance between us. The minute we deviate from simple, practical matters, the conversation lapses imperceptibly into a kind of audio link, a muted love mumble. Our communication, initially meaningful and coherent, turns into a series of fitful exchanges containing neither sentences nor information: little words and sounds meant – I suppose – to keep the line between us open, but which, instead, make all too clear how far apart we are. So we have learned to split the work between us, stick to practical matters, and only speak to one another when necessary.

I've forgotten many of the details of our conversation, but Thomas – who remembers the seventeenth of November as if it were yesterday – has told me that I had spoken in glowing terms of my day's haul and that I had been wondering whether T. & T. Selter should expand its operations to include plates and illustrations. We talked mostly about the practical problems associated with my suggestion, particularly regarding shipping, which would probably be Thomas's job. I felt the idea was worth considering, but Thomas was not so sure.

I don't recall the rest of the conversation, but I do remember that shortly afterwards I had a bath, then I settled myself on the bed in my hotel room and ran an eye over my book list. I also remember that I was quite tired from all the travelling, that I set the alarm on my phone, got undressed and climbed into bed.

I still don't know whether it would be a good idea for T. & T. Selter to expand into scientific plates and illustrations, but I do know that such considerations no longer have any meaning. I know too that Thomas left his parcels at the post office a while ago, that he has been down by the river and past the old watermill, and that he has walked through the woods and will soon be back.

I keep an eye on the rain clouds. The clouds tell me when time is up. The light fades and I see the sky change to dark grey. If I'm sitting in the living room with a book it grows too dark for me to read and I prepare to retreat to the guest room. I sit for a moment listening to the rain and when it intensifies I know that Thomas will soon be back. I get up from the armchair by the window. I go to the kitchen, rinse my cup in the sink, put it in the cupboard and come in here. I usually remember to turn up the heating before I leave the living room. The embers in the grate have long gone cold and when Thomas gets back he'll be wet through from the rain.

But I am not sitting in the living room today. I am sitting at the table in the guest room and the rainclouds are gathering once more. I gaze out at the garden and the apple tree. A couple of apples have fallen onto the grass, a light breeze has blown the autumn leaves almost dry while I've been sitting here, but the tree will soon be wet with rain again. I can still see the birds when they dart about in the faint light. They can tell that rain is on the way, but they haven't yet gone to roost in the hedge.

Darkness falls as I wait for Thomas to go by outside. The writing on the page in front of me becomes hard to read. I've shut the door to the hall and moved away from the window. I usually sit on the bed while I wait for Thomas to get back and I know that first one, then another dark shadow will come along the road at the bottom of the garden. The first shadow is our neighbour. The second is Thomas making his way through the rain. This is the only time I see him: a wet silhouette down by the fence. The rest of the day he is just sounds in the rooms of the house.

Not until Thomas has once again become sounds in the rooms of the house do I turn on a light. I heard his footsteps on the garden path, his key in the lock, and the door being opened and closed. I heard him wipe his feet on the mat and the faint click of the switch when he put on the hall light. I can see light filtering in under the door and I have put on the lamp on the table. My light fills this room and filters out under the door, but it cannot be seen from the hall, mingling as it does to invisibility with the light out there.

I have moved back to the table by the window and before long I hear Thomas's feet on the stairs and the passage again. I hear him in the kitchen and the hall. I hear him open the door facing the road and go out to fetch a leek from the garden and some onions from the shed. I can hear him pulling on the pair of wellingtons by the door. I can hear him walking down the side of the house, and then nothing until he returns with his vegetables. I hear him chopping vegetables for soup. Hear the rattle of the pot on the stove and, once the soup is ready, the scrape of chair legs on the kitchen floor. A little later I hear the gush of water through the pipes as Thomas washes his plate in the kitchen sink, then I hear him putting the plate back in the cupboard before going through to the living room. He spends his evening reading Jocelyn Miron's *Lucid Investigations* and it's almost midnight before he switches off the hall light and goes upstairs, but that is a while off yet, the evening is just beginning. Thomas is getting changed in the bedroom above and I am remembering a long succession of November days that have begun to run together in my mind. There are 121 days to remember. If I can.

To begin with, the eighteenth of November was in no way unusual. I woke up in my hotel room at 7:30 and went down for breakfast half an hour later. I spent the day visiting various antiquarian bookshops in the area around rue Almageste, calling in along the way at Philip Maurel's shop at number 31. Philip's new assistant, whom I had not met before, thought he would be back towards the end of the afternoon so I said I would pop in again around five o'clock. At the different bookshops which we normally buy from when we are in town I found a number of the works I was looking for. I called in at one dealer's in the rue Renart to look at the copy of *Histoire des Eaux Potables* that Thomas had found for sale and that one of our customers had made numerous enquiries about. It was a very nice copy so I bought it on the spot and put it in my bag, to be taken back with me to Clairon-sous-Bois the very next day for Thomas to forward to our impatient customer. At the same dealer's I found a couple of other works which I bought and asked to be sent to Clairon and in another I picked up a copy of Thornton's *The Heavenly Bodies* in good condition and containing two plates only included in this one edition, published in two small printings in 1767.

Just before five o'clock I descended the steps to Philip Maurel's shop again. It was a while since I had seen him, six months, maybe more, and we sat for a while chatting at the big desk in the front part of the shop, with Philip getting up every now and again to serve a customer or to answer the phone. I told him about the house in Clairon-sous-Bois, which he hasn't yet visited, although we've been there for a couple of years now. I spoke about love, about the apple tree in the garden, about leeks and Swiss chard. I told him about the autumn floods, about the river that occasionally overflows its banks and about our business, from which we were at last able to make a living, about the growing demand for illustrated works from the eighteenth century, about the auction and my latest finds. Philip told me about life on the rue Almageste and his new girlfriend, Marie, whom I had met in the shop earlier that day, about the political unrest that autumn and about the high demand for rare and not so rare relics of the past, a trend which he had also observed in his own business.

Philip specialises in coins from Imperial Rome, a business which, when he first set up shop as a very young man, most of his friends regarded as a bit of a joke, but which in recent years has proved to be a lucrative concern. He told me in wonder how, on several occasions, he had been invited to dinner by one of his regular customers only to suddenly find himself at the centre of an interested crowd consisting not only of elderly gentlemen, but also of younger men and women, all eager to hear about Imperial mint regulation, the details of coin pressing techniques or about somewhat suspect Belarusian coin discoveries. He spoke of individuals who would suddenly whisk visitors off through their vast Parisian flats to show off a coin collection, not to the surprise or embarrassment of their guests at this weird hobby, but to their delight, as they studied their host's latest acquisitions intently through powerful magnifying glasses. Philip confessed that he had been rather surprised to see his own quiet passion receiving so much attention. These small metal tokens from bygone ages had apparently become the subject of a new collecting mania – not exactly a wave perhaps, but certainly a growing interest which he was keenly aware of in his business.

We reflected a little on this demand for trophies from the past and I showed Philip my copy of *Histoire des Eaux Potables*. We talked about how keen the buyer had been to get hold of it and wondered why someone would want to buy a book like this. Who buys an over two-hundred-year-old book on the history of drinking water? A collector of some sort, but what exactly his collection consisted of and how the book was to figure in it was hard to guess. I knew nothing about him except his name, his address and the sound of his voice on the phone when he had called for the third time, a few weeks earlier, to enquire about the book. I assumed him to be a middle-aged man and I knew that he had purchased two or three other books from us before, although I couldn't remember which ones.

I still remember how we discussed with a certain irony and detachment this burgeoning interest in the treasures of the past. Although we too could be said to suffer from this same nostalgia or hunger for history or whatever you want to call it, we were both slightly surprised that it was becoming more widespread. I think we almost felt the urge to apologise for our strange interests, which we now evidently shared with more and more people. Well, at least we had managed to make a living out of them. They were our businesses, not a hobby or a fleeting sign of the times. We had our companies, T. & T. Selter and Maurel Numismatique to manage and we felt, I suppose, that we had a somewhat more pragmatic relationship with our inner nostalgist than our customers.

Fortunately Marie, Philip's girlfriend, turned up in the middle of this conversation. Philip introduced us, we exchanged a few words about the current conversation and also about our having met each other earlier in the day. After a little while Marie pulled up a chair and sat down at the counter while Philip went out to pick up some food and a couple of bottles of wine from a nearby shop.

It was one of the first cold November evenings. There had been a shower of rain in the morning, the rest of the day had been cloudy with the occasional sunny spell and it was starting to feel quite chilly in the shop. In the little kitchen at the back, where he had also slept for the first years after opening the shop, Philip had an old gas heater and Marie and I decided to try to light this. Marie wiped a layer of dust off the top and together we managed to manoeuvre the large blue gas cylinder next to the heater into the back of it, attach it and push the heavy appliance through to the shop front and over to the counter. We found a box of matches in a kitchen drawer and lit the gas. By the time Philip got back the shop was warming up nicely. We sat around the counter and spent the next few hours eating, drinking and talking.

What I remember most clearly from that evening is how much I enjoyed sitting there between Philip and Marie. They had a closeness which I could not help but notice. Not the sort of unspoken awareness that shuts other people out, the self-absorption of a couple in the first throes of love who need constantly to make contact by look or touch, nor the fragile intimacy which makes an outsider feel like a disruptive element and gives you the urge to simply leave the lovers alone with their delicate alliance. They had an air of peace about them, Marie and Philip, which reminded me of the time, five years ago, when I first met Thomas. The sudden feeling of sharing something inexplicable, a sense of wonder at the existence of the other – the one person who makes everything simple – a feeling of being calmed and thrown into turmoil at one and the same time. Philip and Marie had clearly decided to spend the rest of their lives together, it was as simple as that, so what could they do but see what the future would bring. Seen in that light, my visit was a perfectly normal occurrence, I was an ingredient in their life together, a colleague of sorts and a friend, married to one of Philip's friends from his early teens. I was not in the way, I was neither a help nor a hindrance, neither an opponent nor a supporter, neither a buyer nor a seller; I was simply a fact in their lives.

I no longer remember the details of the evening's conversation, but I remember the atmosphere in the room. I remember at one point sitting there studying a corner of the big old oak desk we were sitting around, which served as the shop counter. I remember the marks in the wood and a little display of coins set out on it in transparent boxes, which we had to push to one side to make space for the plates and glasses. I also remember the warmth of the room and my accident with the gas heater. It happened some time after we had finished eating. I had pushed my chair back a bit but the heat was almost overpowering, so I got up to move the heater a little further away. I remember Philip had picked up our plates and gone out to the little kitchen at the back of the shop for a corkscrew to open another bottle of wine and I remember saying something about how hot it was and that I would just move the heater slightly. Marie got up, but I had already placed a hand on its upper edge and given it a firm push away from the desk.

While we'd been sitting there the heater had, of course, become red-hot and the metal edge on which I had laid my hand was scorching, so just as the heavy appliance started to shift I felt a sudden, searing pain in my hand. I let out a cry, an expletive probably. Marie came over and managed to move the heater while I stood there, paralysed by the pain for a moment. Having deposited our plates in the kitchen Philip promptly reappeared with a bowl of cold water into which I plunged my hand, and for the rest of the evening I sat like that, with my hand immersed in a bowl of water, although this did little to ease the pain. That was the only unusual thing to happen that night.

I got back to the hotel just before eleven o'clock and shortly after that I called Thomas. He had been engrossed in Jocelyn Miron's book and sounded as though he hadn't been expecting me to call. I don't know whether I had disturbed his reading or whether he was glad of the interruption, but I remember how he filled me in on the central themes of the book and explained the different forms of Enlightenment thinking outlined by Miron. I remember, too, that we discussed the book's rather odd subtitle: *Rises and Falls of Enlightenment Projects*, and then I told him about my visit to Philip Maurel, about his girlfriend Marie and their obvious love for one another, about the growing demand for Imperial coins and my accident with the heater in Philip's shop. Thomas told me that it had rained for most of the day, apart from a break of a few hours in the afternoon. He had taken letters and parcels to the post office and later, when the sun broke through, he had decided to take a walk through the woods and along the river. He had gone as far as the old watermill, thinking that the rain had passed, but on the way home he had been caught in a heavy shower and got absolutely drenched. I remember how we talked about the risk of the river overflowing. He had said that judging by the height of the water, if the weather forecast for the next few days held good then the danger of flooding was over for now. I don't recall all the details of our conversation, but I'm sure I reported on the day's finds, on prices and delivery arrangements, and I know we discussed my plans for the following day, the nineteenth, when I was due to meet Nami Charet at Bibliothèque 18.

Once or twice during our conversation I complained about the still painful burn on my hand and we had a little laugh at my thoughtlessness: it wasn't the first time I had come to grief for not heeding, as Thomas put it, the basic principles of cause and effect. He suggested I get some ice cubes to cool the wound and then we probably exchanged a few inconsequential remarks. I remember one of us observing that we were slipping back into our old familiar audio-link mode, murmurings that accentuated the distance between us, and before we said goodnight a couple of times and hung up I think I promised Thomas I would go straight down to reception for some ice cubes. That was the last time I spoke to Thomas before time fell apart.

I lay awake for a while, half an hour, maybe longer. I had got hold of a bag of ice cubes, laid the ice on the burn and wrapped a towel around my hand. The pain and the cold kept me awake and I tossed and turned a bit, feeling strangely restless in bed, but gradually the chilling effect or the tiredness or whatever it was caused the pain to recede and when I eventually fell asleep it was with a towel full of melting ice cubes around my hand and a small stack of books on the desk in the room: some notes on bird calls, an atlas of spiders, a book on heavenly bodies, a work on the history of drinking water and an encyclopedia of animal anatomy. On a chair next to the bed lay my phone, with the alarm set for 7:30 the next morning. Over the back of the chair hung a dress, a sweater and a pair of tights and on the floor were a pair of ankle boots and a large shoulder bag containing an extra dress, tights, underwear, a purse, a bunch of keys, an almost empty water bottle and a rolled-up umbrella.

I still have the bag beside me on the floor and the books are on the table next to the spare bed. I am no longer in the hotel, but in our house in Clairon-sous-Bois, in the room overlooking the garden. It is evening and it is still the eighteenth of November. Thomas is in the living room, reading, and soon he will switch off the light and check that the doors are locked. He will go upstairs and when he wakes up tomorrow morning his eighteenth of November will have been forgotten.

This is the 121st time I have lived through the eighteenth of November and the burn is still visible as a slender scar on my hand. It started out as an angry, puffy weal. This soon began to weep, then a long, brownish scab formed over it. Little by little the scab loosened and fell off, leaving a shiny pink mark. It can no longer be felt and in a moment, when I turn off the light, it will no longer be seen.

122

I can tell by the sounds. It is the same day. Yet again I have woken in the guest room, and yet again Thomas has gone through his morning routine, the pipes have gushed, the stove and the fridge have emitted their sounds. In a moment Thomas will go out and will soon be back with his bags, and while he is away I will go out to the kitchen and fetch a pack

24

of biscuits or crackers or whatever I can find because I am running low on supplies.

I can hear him getting ready for the November rain. There is a faint chink as he gets out his keys and the swish of fabric across the wallpaper in the hall as he takes his coat off the peg.

I have counted the days. It is my 122nd eighteenth of November. I have come a long way from the seventeenth and I do not know whether I will ever see the nineteenth. But the eighteenth arrives again and again. It arrives and fills the house with sounds. With the sound of a person. He goes about the house and now he is going out.

That is why I began to write. Because I can hear him in the house. Because time has fallen apart. Because I found a pack of paper on the shelf. Because I'm trying to remember. Because the paper remembers. And there may be healing in sentences.

I've seated myself by the window. In front of me is a little pile of papers on which it says that there's someone in the house and that I can hear him moving around. I've written that he's waiting and that he's waiting for me. I've written that time has fallen apart. I'm getting used to the thought. I've written that I'm getting used to the thought and that there is healing in sentences. Maybe.

But it is still the same day and in a little while, when I have collected a few supplies from the kitchen, when I have been to the toilet and brushed my teeth, once I have closed the door and settled myself in this room again I will hear Thomas return with his shopping. I will hear him take things out of his bags and put them away. I will hear the fridge being opened and bumping against the worktop. I will hear him in the office upstairs, in the kitchen and in the hall. I will hear the sound of a hand or a sleeve brushing the wall on the stairs and the little thud on the floorboards as he sets down letters and parcels in the hall.

It dawned on me at breakfast. I had woken up in my room at the Hôtel du Lison shortly before half-past seven with a damp towel beside me and a burn that no longer hurt very much. I had a quick shower and went down for breakfast. I ordered coffee, got myself something from the buffet and took this and a newspaper back to my table, but a quick scan of the front page was enough to tell me that it was the one I'd read the day before. When I went out to reception and asked for that morning's paper I was told that the one I had in my hand was that morning's newspaper, that it was the eighteenth of November and that the day before had been the seventeenth. Even when I know I am right I seldom bother to argue such points, so I picked up another of the previous day's papers, returned to my table and finished my coffee.

It was only when one of the hotel's other guests dropped a

piece of bread on the floor that I began to worry. Not because I don't know that this sort of thing happens again and again in hotels all over the world, but because the same guest had dropped a piece of bread at that same spot the day before. It was a slice of white bread, the same size as the one he'd dropped the day before and its fall occurred at the same speed, a gently swerving descent, slow enough to show that this was a fairly light piece of bread. The hotel guest's actions were also identical. There was the same hesitation as he bent down for the bread and then, once he had picked it up, seemed unable to decide what to do with it. He was clearly torn between two codes of conduct: one which said you don't throw away good food, and another which said that food which falls from society's platters, baskets and plates is to be regarded as waste. Now I observed the same discreet movement as on the previous day when, after a glance around the room he decided to slip the bread into a wastebin and take a croissant instead.

The moment I saw this hesitant action I knew that I was witnessing a repetition. I didn't know that there would be yet another eighteenth of November the next day and then another and another, but I knew that something was wrong.

I immediately went out to check the date on the papers at the nearest newsstand, then to a cashpoint where I made a withdrawal on my credit card and shortly afterwards I called in at two different hotels to take a look at the calendar in reception, not because I was in any doubt, but solely because I had to do something to handle my confusion. The dates on the newspapers, on my cashpoint receipt and on the hotel calendars confirmed that it was indeed the eighteenth of November. The weather, too, was the same. It had rained while I was having breakfast, but the sky had now cleared. I walked around the wet streets and saw the first shops opening up. It was going to be a cool day with some cloud and occasional sunny spells.

Back at the hotel I called Thomas, on the pretext that I had forgotten the time of my appointment with Nami Charet at Bibliothèque 18 in Clichy. This confirmed for me that for Thomas too it was the eighteenth of November. My appointment was on the nineteenth. Tomorrow, he said, at eleven a.m., and it was clear that as far as he was concerned this was the year's first and only eighteenth of November, a freshly opened, almost untouched day. It was the day after the seventeenth of November and the day before the nineteenth when I would be coming home as planned.

From our brief conversation it soon became plain that everything I had told him the evening before about my day was gone and that he had no recollection of his own rainy November day either. As far as he was concerned he had taken no letters or parcels to the post office. He had not been down by any river, he had not got drenched by any shower of rain and he had no memory of our telephone conversation on the evening of the eighteenth. There was no information stored in his memory banks on my visit to Philip Maurel's, no Marie, no gas heater, no burn or ice cubes. There was no record of *Eaux Potables* or *Heavenly Bodies*, no discussions about Jocelyn Miron's distinctions. Only our earlier conversation. From the previous evening. The seventeenth.

Afterwards I sat there in my hotel room, on the unmade bed, with my back against the wall and my phone beside me. I had kept my questions light. I hadn't wanted to worry him, I simply wanted to know whether it was just me, and it was. Thomas had had no eighteenth of November.

It must have been about fifteen minutes, maybe half an hour, before my eye fell on the books. The little pile had grown smaller. The books from the eighteenth were gone. On the table in the room lay the volumes I had bought on the seventeenth: *Atlas des Araigneées*, *The Anatomy of Animals* and *Musick of Nature's Birds*. But *Histoire des Eaux Potables* and *The Heavenly Bodies* were no longer there.

Half an hour after, I went down to the two antiquarian bookshops where I had bought these works. One of them was not yet open, but a few minutes later, when I opened the door of the other shop I saw Thornton's *Heavenly Bodies* right away: there on the shelf behind the counter, in the very spot from which the bookseller had taken it the day before. The bookseller, whom I had met several times at auctions and in her shop on the rue Renart, clearly did not remember me being in the shop the previous day or selling me the book. I bought it again, apologised for being in such a hurry, returned to the other bookshop, which was now open, and asked the owner if he had the copy of *Histoire des Eaux Potables* which Thomas had asked him to set aside. He promptly produced the book and asked after Thomas, to whom he believed he had spoken the day before. *Yesterday*, as he said. Then he mentioned three other titles which he had also shown me on my visit the previous day and which I had already bought and asked to be sent to Clairon. I didn't buy them this time around, but paid for *Histoire des Eaux Potables*, put it in my bag alongside Thornton's *Heavenly Bodies* and walked back to the hotel.

On the way I called in at Philip's shop where his assistant, whom I now knew as Marie, told me that Philip had just gone out but that he would be back in the late afternoon. She gave no sign of recognising me and I didn't feel like insisting that we knew one another.

On the counter I noticed a Roman sestertius that Philip had shown me the previous evening. It lay in a transparent box along with two other Roman coins. It was a copper coin with the head of Emperor Antoninus Pius on the one side and on the reverse an elaborate relief of the goddess Annona, with two ears of corn in one hand and a grain measure in the other. Marie let me look at the details through a magnifying glass and explained that the grain measure – a modius, she called it – indicated that this was Annona, the divine personification of the grain supply vital to imperial retention of power in Rome. Like many other emperors Antoninus Pius needed to import enormous quantities of grain to avoid unrest and Annona had been an important goddess, Marie said. As she was sure I knew, she added after a pause. I nodded and for a moment I sensed a kind of familiarity, a glimmer of recognition, perhaps. But I must have been mistaken. It was probably just wishful thinking.

I bought the sestertius and asked to have it gift-wrapped. While Marie was placing the coin in a blue-grey box and wrapping it, I wandered around the shop. In the front room stood the big desk which we had sat around the evening before and at which Marie was now wrapping my sestertius. On the wall behind the desk were lots of drawers and cabinets containing coins and on the walls in the room next door Philip had a wide assortment of his stock displayed in glass cases. I stepped into the room and so as not to seem too obvious I turned to the left and slowly worked my way along the cases lining the walls, on which the coins were arranged in chronological order. The first case held a variety of pre-Roman coins, mostly Greek, and a small collection of Indian and Chinese coins, a selection Philip was planning to expand, but which was currently still placed out on the fringes of the Roman Empire. Under a long window offering a view up to the street stood a low bookcase holding catalogues and books; on the other walls were cabinets of Roman coins arranged according to the various periods and coinage reforms. I crossed to the ones containing coins from the Roman Empire and studied Philip's simple display, which made the line of emperors seem like a straightforward chronological progression, a succession of faces, seamlessly following on from one another, binding the era together. This tour of the display cases was a familiar one, a round I had made many times before. The Roman emperors and empresses, their gods and goddesses and the tiny symbols and objects designed to tell us who they were, reassured me and gave me time to consider the situation.

Past the last glass case, containing pieces from the time around the fall of the Western Roman Empire and a handful of Byzantine coins, the door to the shop's back room was open. Ranged along one wall in there were the kitchen worktop, a fridge and a sink and on the other side was a run of cupboards. Beyond the cupboards were some boxes, and it was behind these boxes that the gas heater had stood the day before.

I waited for a moment and then, while Marie was answering the phone, I nipped into the back room. Sure enough: at the very end, tucked well into a corner, were a blue gas cylinder and a heater covered in an undisturbed layer of dust.

The burn mark on my hand still hurt a little, but I had grown so used to the pain that I never really gave it a thought unless I happened to bump my hand or made a sudden move.

As long as I kept my hand still the pain was merely a faint background noise in my nervous system, nothing to speak of, a minor injury, a burn from a dusty heater that hadn't been used since last winter.

I hurried back to Marie, paid for my sestertius and left the shop. The coin was for Thomas. I had not decided whether I would go back home to him straight away or whether I would wait. According to my original plan I should now have been on my way to Bibliothèque 18, but that had been on the assumption that, during the night, it would have become the nineteenth of November. This had not happened, so instead I went to a pharmacy and bought a box of burn plasters and a tube of antiseptic ointment.

Back at the hotel I took a big rectangular plaster out of the box from the pharmacy and put it over the burn, which had become slightly swollen and inflamed. Then I called Thomas. I told him about the rift in time I had discovered, but which no one else seemed to have noticed, and I confessed that this had been my real reason for calling him a couple of hours earlier. I didn't want to worry him, but I now saw nothing else for it but to inform him of the problem. Over the next few minutes I related the events of the eighteenth of November, including countless details that are no longer clear in my memory. I told him of my visits to the antiquarian bookshops, of the books I had now bought for the second time, of my visit to Marie and the dusty gas heater in the back-shop. I did not tell him about the sestertius I had bought for him, but I believe that most of the other events of both my first and my second eighteenth of November were reported in a long monologue to which Thomas listened almost without comment or question.

Today, what I remember most clearly from that conversation is the imbalance that suddenly arose between us when I referred to our conversation from the evening before. Thomas began to ask questions, with a note of concern in his voice. He understood that he had been part of my eighteenth of November, that he had spoken to me and that he had told me about his day. I could describe his day, I could describe the weather and events of which he no longer had any recollection.

He didn't doubt that I was telling the truth. He had spoken to me and had forgotten it. That was what scared him. It was one thing for me to have encountered a fracture in the normal progression of time, but the idea that he had played a part in my day and that he had had conversations and done things he could not remember obviously gave him the same feelings of faintness and unease which I had had when I saw that slice of bread drifting floorwards. That strange moment when the ground under one's feet falls away and all at once it feels as though all predictability can be suspended, as though an existential red alert has suddenly been triggered, a quiet state of panic which prompts neither flight nor cries for help, and does not call for police, fire brigade or ambulance. It is as if this emergency response mechanism is there on stand-by at

the back of the mind, like an undertone, not normally aud-
ible, but kicking in the moment one is confronted with the
unpredictability of life, the knowledge that everything can
change in an instant, that something which cannot happen
and which we absolutely do not expect, is nonetheless a possibility. That time stands still. That gravity is suspended. That
the logic of the world and the laws of nature break down. That
we are forced to acknowledge that our expectations about the
constancy of the world are on shaky ground. There are no
guarantees and behind all that we ordinarily regard as certain
lie improbable exceptions, sudden cracks and inconceivable
breaches of the usual laws.

It seems so odd to me now, how one can be so unsettled by
the improbable. When we know that our entire existence is
founded on freak occurrences and improbable coincidences.
That we wouldn't be here at all if it weren't for these curious
twists of fate. That there are human beings on what we call
our planet, that we can move around on a rotating sphere in a
vast universe full of inconceivably large bodies comprised of
elements so small that the mind simply cannot comprehend
how small and how many they are. That in this unfathom-
able vastness, these infinitesimal elements are still able to hold
themselves together. That we manage to stay afloat. That we
exist at all. That each of us has come into being as only one of
untold possibilities. The unthinkable is something we carry
with us always. It has already happened: we are improbable,
we have emerged from a cloud of unbelievable coincidences.

Anyone would think that this knowledge would equip us in some small way to face the improbable. But the opposite appears to be the case. We have grown accustomed to living with that knowledge without feeling dizzy every morning, and instead of moving around warily and tentatively, in constant amazement, we behave as if nothing has happened, take the strangeness of it all for granted and get dizzy if life shows itself as it truly is: improbable, unpredictable, remarkable.

And then it kicks in, the emergency response. And I could tell, as I sat there in my hotel room, still dazed by having witnessed the repeated fall of a slice of bread, that that was what had happened to Thomas. I could tell by his voice. The quiet panic when he realised what had happened and his faltering attempts to come up with a reasonable explanation. It wasn't a problem with the line. It was the ground under his feet falling away, his emergency response being triggered, his first-aid box being unpacked. The door opening onto a world in which everything can be subject to change. A time falling apart, a day repeating itself, experiences disappearing from memory without a trace, dust returning to places from which one knows it had been wiped away.

Usually, things close up again: it was a mistake. A simple explanation is found for the freak occurrence: our eyes deceived us, our memories were playing tricks on us, we had got things mixed up, got the days wrong. There is solid ground under our feet again, the incomprehensible makes sense after all, it was an optical illusion or a slip of the mind, it was a dream or a misunderstanding, the world is set to rights, the dizziness passes, we can breathe more easily.

But not this time. I had seen a piece of bread fall two days in a row and there was no misunderstanding. I had seen Marie wipe a layer of dust off a heater which was now every bit as dusty as it had been when we found it in the back room of Philip Maurel's shop. I had spoken to Thomas. He had told me about his day. I remembered his eighteenth of November, Thomas did not, but we both knew that I was telling the truth. I was not mistaken. There was no mix-up, no confusion. I knew I was right and Thomas saw no reason to doubt me.

Thomas said he would have another look at the day. I could still hear the concern in his voice. He seemed eager to end the conversation. He was going to go out for a walk and would call me back in a little while. He called just over half an hour later, by which time he had checked the internet, several newspapers, two banks and an office supplies shop, and was now sitting in Café La Petite Échelle in the centre of Clairon. A light rain was falling, it was a little after two o'clock, he had just heard a carillon ring out from the steeple of the church next door to the café and he was sure that it was the eighteenth of November.

He could not explain it, but the facts of the day were simple: I had woken to the same eighteenth of November two days in a row and everything that was going on around me was happening exactly as it had the day before, it was a replica of the day I already had stored in my memory. Thomas, on the other hand, felt no sense of recognition and could not detect the slightest sign that he might have lived through this day once before. All he remembered was our conversation on the seventeenth, which he found it hard not to refer to as *yesterday*.

We spent a few minutes debating various possible explanations: hallucinations or memory blips, misunderstandings or misinterpretations, temporal loops or parallel universes, but we could get none of these to make sense. Neither of us believed in the possibility of portals to unknown dimensions and the most obvious explanation was, of course, that I had imagined the whole thing, that it was a hallucination, a rather too vivid fantasy, a dream. But that my entire eighteenth of November should have been a dream, a figment of my imagination, a hallucination, was not convincing: figments of the imagination don't leave burn marks, you don't dream a whole morning newspaper and you don't normally encounter an exact replica of your hallucinations in the breakfast room of a three-star Parisian hotel. We were baffled. The one thing we could say for sure was that I was looking at a world which had returned to its starting point during the night, it had jumped back a day, to unfold again in exactly the same way as the day before.

It was hard to see what was to be done. We weighed up various solutions: I could stay where I was and see what the day would bring, or I could go home straight away, to Thomas, to the only person who, at this point, was affected by this rift in time and, in all probability, the only person with whom I could share this bizarre phenomenon without being met with doubt or being regarded as a mad woman, a weirdo or, quite simply, a liar. Thomas could, of course, also come to Paris so that we could investigate the matter together or wait for the day to become normal again, but he didn't think this would solve the problem and the longer we talked the more it became clear that the only solution was for me to return home. There wasn't much we could do here and now. I would have to go back.

We hung up, promising to see each other soon. I calmly packed my things. I gathered up the books, wrapped them carefully and put them in my bag, put on my coat and set off for the station, arriving there half an hour later. After a wait of almost an hour I boarded a train to Lille, where I changed trains and carried on to Clairon-sous-Bois.

It was dark when I got off the train in Clairon. I had tried to call and book a taxi but couldn't get through so I decided to walk the nigh on two kilometres from the train station to our house. It had started raining while I was on the train, the wind had risen slightly and I walked out into the downpour with my open umbrella in one hand and my bag over the other shoulder. It was about seven o'clock, there was water on the road, it was dark and cold and the rain eased up for only a few seconds at a time. The burn on my hand, which I had not been all that aware of on the train, was again sending a searing stab of pain through me with every step I took. I could feel the plaster loosening in the rain and every now and again I had to stop and try to fix it back in place or swap my bag and umbrella over, but it made no difference, the pain simply shifted momentarily and then returned.

Oddly enough, there was something soothing about that journey from the station to our house. As if the walking befitted the situation, and the cold, the discomfort and the pain of the burn reflected my inner turmoil. It wasn't only the sense that something had gone wrong, not only the sensations of cold and unease and discomfort. There was also a feeling that somewhere out there a solution was to be found; a conviction that if I simply kept walking through the cold and the wet, if I endured the pain in my hand, if I pressed on with a firm grip on the umbrella and with the heavy bag over my shoulder, if I plodded on through the rain, one step at a time, I would make it through, to a house, to a warm room and to Thomas, waiting there. I was alone, assailed by water and cold, with a burned hand and a bag full of books over my shoulder, but the situation was not hopeless and as long as shelter from the rain, dry clothes and Thomas awaited at the end of my journey a solution could be found. I just had to get through this walk in the rain.

When I got there everything was as I had expected. The street lamp outside the house sent the familiar shadows of the bushes in the front garden falling across the wet wall of the house. The vegetable plot lay in semi-darkness and the white door of the garden shed could be seen from the street. The flagstone path led me from the street to the front door, just as it always did. It was November, it was raining, I had been in Bordeaux, and gone from there to Paris, I had called in on Philip Maurel, had bought books and come home after two days as planned. The only irregularity was that I had not kept my appointment with Nami Charet and that there had been no nineteenth of November. A minor variation, an error in a sequence of numbers. A rift in time, a fault I could not immediately fix, the extent of which I could not yet gauge and which I could not therefore call either a bagatelle or a disaster, but which at that moment, as I walked up the front path to the house, was reduced to a detail that could wait.

Over the days that have passed since my walk through the rain that minor fault in time has grown greater: a calendar error that can no longer be ignored. Thinking back, I can still recall the feeling from that evening when I walked home from the station. For a fleeting moment I could see this rift in time as a mere detail, a problem that could be solved, a trek through cold and rain that would soon be over, but then I remember that it is not some detail that can simply be dismissed. The error did not disappear, it grew bigger and I don't know how to erase it.

Thomas waved to me from the kitchen window as soon as I appeared in the light of the street lamp. Our eyes met for a second and he raised a hand that stopped in mid-air as he turned and hurried to the door. We met in the doorway. I shook the raindrops off my umbrella and Thomas quickly drew me into the warm and dry, into the house, relieving me first of my umbrella and my bag, then of my coat and there we stood with only a single day between us, as if I had merely been away on a trip, not a perfectly ordinary trip, something had changed, there was an anxious undertone to our meeting, nonetheless I felt I had reached safety, as if an accident had just been avoided, a hotel fire, a car crash, a train wreck that had narrowly passed me by. I had escaped danger and come home. I was filled with a sense of relief, the ache in my shoulder eased, the pain in my hand receded and I could feel Thomas's shirt getting damp from the rain I had brought into the house.

Once I was in the hall and had taken off my boots, Thomas went up to the bedroom to fetch a warm sweater for me. I carried my wet bag into the living room, took out the books which, luckily, had not been damaged by the rain and put them on the table. I unearthed dry clothes from the bottom of the bag, changed, pulled the sweater Thomas had brought me over my dress and sat down in one of the two armchairs by the living-room window. Thomas made tea, carried two cups through to the living room and took the other chair. And there we sat, in our armchairs, with a low table between us, relieved to be together, and chatted about the weather, the books, Philip and Marie, my accident with the gas heater and my burn, which I showed him by pulling the large plaster aside. It was now red and seeping but no longer particularly painful, not now, as I sat there peacefully in the warmth.

We kept the conversation neutral. I scrupulously avoided using words we would interpret differently, terms such as *yesterday* or *the day before yesterday*. I said *today* and *the seventeenth* and *the evening I went to see Philip* and in this way we managed to talk about my trip without too many misunderstandings.

I gave Thomas the Roman sestertius. I told him I had bought it the morning I visited Philip's shop to check the unused gas heater. Thomas is not really a collector, nor is he especially interested in the worth or rarity of the coins, but over the years he has, nonetheless, built up a notable little collection. As far as I can tell, there is no system to the selection of items for his collection, which he keeps in a sturdy cardboard box. It consists not only of coins, but also of some postage stamps, a few small engravings and a couple of pocket-sized illustrated books.

This collection, if one can call it that, is one of the few things Thomas still has from the days before we knew each other. That and the house, of course, which was left to him by his paternal grandfather a year or two after we met, and the garden, which still looks like the garden Thomas played in as a little boy. We took over a house full of things which he had known since his childhood: the two armchairs, the black-and-white rug in the living room, the cups on the little table between us, the desk in the office upstairs, the tools in the shed, the bookcase in the living room and the old hi-fi, which still works. The rest of our furniture comes from my flat in Brussels, which Thomas moved into not long after we met. He brought with him several cases of antiquarian books – the nucleus of what was to become T. & T. Selter – and the box containing his little assortment of objects, which was where I suppose I thought the Roman sestertius belonged.

We stayed in the living room for most of the evening. I was back. We were together again. Sitting there that night with our teacups, the world seemed almost normal. Still, though, it was impossible to avoid the feeling of unease brought on by this glitch in time. Over those hours we approached the subject from different angles, but we could not come up with an explanation or a solution. Thomas, wanting to reassure me or to reassure himself perhaps, thought the problem might simply go away. At one point he remarked casually that time must surely always revert to its eternal forward progression. People have always had to allow for certain disruptions in life, rivers flooding their banks, road accidents, twisted ankles, hard winters or droughts, but in the end, he said, here we were, as if nothing had happened. No one had died, no one had been hurt.

I was worried. For safety's sake I took the books I had brought home from Paris up to the bedroom with me when we went to bed that night. I laid them at the foot of the bed before we slipped under the duvet and snuggled up together, though with no talk of our plans for the next day as there would normally have been. Maybe we thought the chances of everything going back to a normal time-scale were greater if we acted as if nothing had happened.

Soon I could tell that Thomas was falling asleep. I could hear his breathing and glimpse the outline of his face and I think I saw him open his eyes for a second. I am no longer sure what I saw there in the dark, but what I remember now is a fleeting glance which I can only describe as faintly reproachful, as if it was not time, but me, that was failing him and throwing his world out of kilter.

He immediately closed his eyes again. I don't know if he fell asleep straight away, but after a few minutes, when I was sure he was sleeping, I disengaged his arm and very gently edged away.

I was still worried. I could feel the books at the foot of the bed and on impulse I pulled *Histoire des Eaux Potables* and *The Heavenly Bodies* out of the pile down there and put them under my pillow before I too fell asleep.

The next morning I woke before Thomas and at first everything seemed normal. I could feel the bedclothes against my skin, Thomas lying next to me. I was aware of a coolness in the air, the pale light from the window. For a while, a few minutes maybe, or maybe just seconds, I felt I was greeting a perfectly ordinary morning – a well-known sense of normality. I was awake, Thomas was asleep.

A moment later, though, it dawned on me that I had not simply woken up in bed next to Thomas on a perfectly ordinary morning. At first it was merely a flicker of unease, a feeling that something wasn't right, that I had forgotten something, that something had escaped me, and only when I felt the books under my pillow did I realise what had been troubling me. Details of the eighteenth of November followed the books into my morning and at that same moment I remembered that I had been in Paris, that I had woken to the eighteenth of November instead of the nineteenth as expected, and that I had returned home through the rain, that I had talked to Thomas, who was now asleep in bed beside me, and that I had put two books under my pillow before I went to sleep, the two books which I had now retrieved. I felt around at the foot of the bed and found the three other books, picked them up and carefully lifted the whole pile off the bed and onto the floor. Then I reached for a sweater that was hanging over the back of a chair, pulled it over my nightdress and went down to the kitchen.

The situation was still unclear. It might be the eighteenth, it might be the nineteenth. It might even be the twentieth of November. I had no idea and I was in no rush to find out. I made breakfast. I boiled eggs, made toast, mixed a batch of muesli, divided it between two bowls and set them on the tray. There were a couple of apples from the garden in a bowl on the worktop, I took one of them, cut off a few brown spots, diced the apple and sprinkled it equally over the two bowls of muesli. I spun out the time, I made coffee, but then had second thoughts and made a pot of tea as well. I got out cups and plates, knives and spoons. I fetched butter, cheese, jam, honey, milk and piled all of this onto the tray, which was now full to the brim. I took the tray upstairs, left it on the landing and went back down to get the pots of coffee and tea, carried them up, set them down on the landing, picked up the breakfast tray again and carried it into the bedroom.

When I came in with the tray Thomas was awake. He was clearly taken aback. As far as he was concerned it was the eighteenth of November, not for the second or third time, but for the first time. The day before had been the seventeenth. The day after would be the nineteenth, the day when I was due back from my trip. That I was already back and standing there in the bedroom with an overflowing breakfast tray came as a surprise to him.

I set the tray on the bed, collected the pots of coffee and tea from the landing and placed them on the bedside table before climbing into bed with Thomas. I told him about my visit to Paris, about my homecoming and our evening together. He checked the dates and times on his phone, but all this told him was that it was now the eighteenth of November and that the time was 9:07 a.m. He could see that we had spoken on the seventeenth. There was no trace of the eighteenth and he remembered nothing of it. No telephone conversations, no homecomings, no wet umbrellas or coats could be called up from his memory. There were no books brought home, no guarded conversations or reassuring sentences. I saw the worry in his eyes when I described how I had walked through the rain from the station to our house and how he had seen me from the kitchen window, had started a wave which he never finished because he had turned away. I showed him the way he had raised his hand, I told him how we had met at the door, how everything had seemed almost normal and I was quick to point out that I was back now, we were in bed, with breakfast on a tray, we were together, no one had died, no one had been hurt. True, the chunks of apple I had sprinkled over the muesli were starting to go brown and the hot drinks had surrendered some of their warmth to the morning air, but that was all. We were together, we could have breakfast together, we could spend the day in each other's company.

While we ate we tentatively addressed the question as to what had happened. Thomas was not sure. He thought we should see how things went. I think he needed to get used to the idea. Or maybe he was hoping that my memories of the previous two eighteenths of November would suddenly vanish and a more acceptable explanation for my return would present itself. But I already knew what the day had in store. It was the same day, the third of its kind.

After breakfast Thomas checked the date on the computer in the office, he read the news, the weather forecast and flood warnings, but everything pointed to a perfectly ordinary eighteenth of November. A little later he suggested that we go for a walk, do the shopping and maybe stroll down to the river. I felt it might be better to wait till the afternoon when it cleared up, as Thomas had told me it would, even though it didn't exactly look like it from the weather forecast, and sure enough, at quarter past three the rain stopped, the clouds began to disperse and the sun came out. We wrapped up warmly, remembered our umbrellas and went for our usual walk through the woods and down to the river. We walked down to the disused watermill and carried on along the path by the river which, despite the amount of rain that had fallen in November, had not yet broken its banks. We walked on through the woods and into town, where we did our shopping at the market before heading back to the house.

I had gathered together the five books I had bought in Bordeaux and Paris and put them in a rucksack I often use when I go shopping. It was a kind of intuitive safety measure which I could not really explain to Thomas. I had the feeling that the books would disappear if I didn't keep them near me and when Thomas offered to carry them I promptly refused. On the way back through town I couldn't resist peering through the bank windows at the calendar on the wall and further on I also had to stop and check the date at a cashpoint. At the post office in the rue Pareillet I felt compelled to check the date on the screen of the stamp-vending machine, as if seeking a loophole in the host of signs that the day was repeating itself. But wherever I looked the date was the same. There was no doubt. It was the eighteenth of November for the third time.

The clouds began to gather, the pale-grey sky which had occasionally cleared to reveal patches of blue, was now darkening. A light drizzle fell on the way back, but we made it home before the heavens opened. Not long afterwards, when the sky was totally dark and the rain was bucketing down we saw our neighbour walking past the fence at the bottom of the garden. He turned the corner and jogged down to his house, opened his gate and disappeared from view. I took the books out of my rucksack and placed them on the table in the living room, and when the rain slackened off Thomas fetched some wood from the shed and lit a fire.

We made love on the living-room floor. We have always had need of time together. We are not one of those couples that has to have time apart, to miss and rediscover one another, to go away then be reunited in a collision of love. Distance, leave-takings and reunions are not what bind us to one another. For us it has always been about the days together, day after day, night after night, again and again. There is a tension that grows between us, a force field that intensifies as the day goes on until often, after a long day together, we will suddenly start to undress one another. Now we lay on the floor, on the black-and-white rug while the rain went on falling outside.

Our love has always been microscopic. It is something in the cells, some molecules, some compounds outside of our control, which collide in the air around us, sound waves that form unique harmonies when we speak, it happens at the atomic level or that of even smaller particles. There are no precipices or distances in our relationship. It is something else, a sort of cellular vertigo, a sort of electricity or magnetism, or maybe it's a chemical reaction, I don't know. It is something that occurs in the air between us, a feeling that is heightened when we are in each other's company. Maybe we are a weather system – condensation and evaporation: we are together, we look at one another, we touch one another, we condense, we come together, we make love, we fall asleep, we wake and revert to our strange bond, a quiet weather system with no natural disasters. Or a weather system which, until the eighteenth of November saw no disasters.

That evening I took the books upstairs and laid them at the foot of the bed. After a moment's hesitation I thought better of this and again tucked *Heavenly Bodies* and *Les Eaux Potables* safely under my pillow. They had come through our day unscathed but I felt no desire to experiment. Early on in the day I had realised that the Roman sestertius had disappeared, but I hadn't mentioned this to Thomas, possibly hoping that it would turn up. I had looked for it in the most obvious places: in my bag, on the table in the living room, on the desk in the office, but it was nowhere to be found.

I told Thomas about the sestertius. He could not remember, of course, what we had done with it the night before, but now we hunted for it in all the places where one of us might have put a Roman coin. First Thomas checked whether he had put it with his collection in the office, but it wasn't there, nor had it been tucked into a drawer, left on the corner of a shelf or set down on a windowsill in the bedroom.

I was – and still am – convinced that the sestertius must have returned to Philip Maurel's shop, just as the books had returned to their shelves on that first night. I have considered going back to Paris to find out, but for now I will stay where I am. I won't go to Paris and I won't go into the living room to join Thomas, who went up the stairs to the office a few minutes ago and returned to the living room shortly afterwards carrying a notepad in which he will scribble the odd comment on the book he is reading. Evening has come. Yet another eighteenth of November is almost over. I have been sitting by the window for most of the day, in a room that sheds its light over the wet garden, and I am going nowhere.

We didn't find the sestertius, of course. While I checked the chest of drawers in the bedroom for a second time, Thomas sat in bed, trying to understand the mechanics of the eighteenth of November, but the logic of the day was hard to see.

Some things disappeared, but not all. My bag and my clothes had not disappeared, nor had the books bought on the seventeenth, and even the two books which I had bought on the eighteenth, which had vanished from my room at the Hôtel du Lison first time around and had to be purchased again, had stayed with us. They had been under my pillow at night and kept under observation all day, and they were still there. The sestertius, on the other hand, was nowhere to be found.

A minute later, when I turned to Thomas in the midst of a lengthy disquisition on the inconsistencies of time and a rundown of the day's events, it was to find that he now seemed amused by the situation, as if, having had the day to come to terms with the idea, he was now starting to regard the peculiar behaviour of time as a joke that had entered our life. By the time I curled up next to him under the duvet his anxiety of the morning had gone, to be replaced by this sudden hilarity, and before we settled down to sleep – to be on the safe side, as he said – he made a short speech, addressed first to the books under my pillow, then to the books at the foot of the bed, asking them to stay a little while longer, and then he snuggled up close to me, put his arms around me and asked me, too, to stay till the next day, whatever day it might be, or better still, the day after that – and preferably forever, in fact. Soon after that he was asleep and minutes later I must have fallen asleep myself.

It is the thought of such moments that occasionally moves me to get up and go over to the door into the hall, but I don't open it because I remember that first I would have to explain my presence, that I now have 122 days to account for, that I would yet again have to see the anxiety in Thomas's eyes and quickly add that no one is dead or injured, that it is only time that has fallen apart, and so I stop and stay in here. It would take all night for the absurdity of the situation to even begin to cheer us up. As if this hilarity lies deep down, as if it first has to well up to the surface through layers of disquiet and doubt, through questions and a lack of answers, like bubbles of gas trapped in permafrost that need time to thaw out.

I am getting used to the idea. I am trapped in a single November day, but I am at home and Thomas is in the living room, engrossed in the fourth chapter of Jocelyn Miron's *Lucid Investigations*. I doubt if I am in his thoughts right now, but if I am he will imagine that I am at the Hôtel du Lison, or that I am with Philip Maurel in his shop. He will not be expecting me to call him this evening, probably not until tomorrow morning or possibly later, after I have been to see Nami Charet at Bibliothèque 18 and am on a train, heading back to Clairon. I expect Thomas to sit there reading for a little while longer, putting down his book every now and again to scribble a few words on his notepad, then tearing that sheet off the pad and slipping it in at the end of the fourth chapter. That done, I expect him to switch off the living-room light, check that the doors are locked, first the front door and then the back, that he will then switch off the hall light, go upstairs and get into bed in the room above. I imagine that I will soon put out the light in this room, go to bed and wake tomorrow to the eighteenth of November # 123.

123

The next morning – on my fourth eighteenth of November – it was Thomas who woke first. I felt his hand on my shoulder, I heard the delight in his voice together with a touch of confusion as he asked when I had got home and how I could be back when I had spoken to him only the evening before from my hotel in Paris. I sat up in bed and after a few seconds I remembered what had happened. He repeated his question and for a moment I thought that he meant the conversation we had had after my visit to Philip Maurel's shop and that he now suddenly recalled his first eighteenth of November, but it was the seventeenth he was talking about. What he remembered was our conversation before I went to bed at the hotel on the night I arrived from Bordeaux. Again, Thomas had woken for the first time to the eighteenth of November and everything that had happened in between had been wiped out. Gone was his rainy November day in Clairon-sous-Bois. Gone our telephone conversation after my visit to Philip Maurel. My return home on the eighteenth of November had been erased. Our breakfast in bed on the third eighteenth of November had faded from his memory, as had the conversations we had had throughout the day, our walk through town, our lovemaking on the living-room rug, our search for the lost sestertius and the speech he had made to the books on the bed. It was the eighteenth of November for the fourth time and I already knew that this day would not stick in his memory either.

Again, I told Thomas what had happened and again I saw his delight at my return give way to disquiet. Once more I tried to answer the questions he put to me, but could give him no reasonable explanation.

Over the days that followed I woke every morning to the same vague sense of normality that I had woken to on the morning after my return. On a couple of occasions Thomas woke me, surprised to find me lying fast asleep beside him, but usually I woke first. I woke up gradually. Initially, simply with a feeling of being home, in a state between sleeping and waking, a hazy awareness. Like waking to something that hasn't quite taken shape and feeling, for a few moments, that everything is the same as always. Like mornings in strange rooms when you think you have woken up in your own bed, until you realise that the door is in the wrong place, the bedding is unfamiliar, the room is different. Or like the mornings of childhood that present themselves as perfectly ordinary days, but then turn out to be Christmas Day or a birthday. Or conversely: you stretch, preparing for an ordinary morning, only then to discover that you have woken to a worry and unease that had been absent during the night.

That is how the days began: with an undefined morning. There is the grey light from the window. There is the birdsong, the sound of rain. There is the feel of the bed linen against my skin, the faint sound of the wind in the trees, a soft sighing in the morning air. I remember it as a world with almost no depth of focus, not like in a dream, more as if part of one's consciousness has been closed off: you are awake, you are conscious of the world around you, you are vision and hearing, a kind of listening post, but where only those things closest to are perceptible, everything else recedes into the background and fades away, as if the day were trying to arrive unclothed, neutral, devoid of attributes. It is just a morning, the simplest possible morning.

It lasts for a moment. I float in the morning fog, I am aware of the room around me, I can feel Thomas stir, asleep or almost awake, my hand reaching out, the dawn light, the furniture in the room, the door leading out to the stairs, and little by little the details come into focus, memory kicks in, I remember what has happened, that time has fallen apart but that the days continue to pass. Five days, six or seven, eight, ten or twelve, and I realise that my morning has been broached and the day is becoming yet another eighteenth of November.

I don't know what is going on. Whether time is switched off at night, whether past and future disappear during slumber and are not invoked again until one wakes. Or whether it is the words that are erased, leaving only the outlines of things. Maybe it is language that shuts down, so one wakes up wordless or with words only for the most immediate concepts:

morning, now, here, awake, light. Maybe one wakes without sentences. Or with the simplest sentences, which unfold as one wakes up. Now it is morning. Here is a day. I am awake.

I don't know. But every morning the same thing happened. I woke up in bed next to Thomas, to the grey light filtering through the curtain, the bedding, the faint sound of rain and wind and a hazy impression of morning that gradually turned into yet another eighteenth of November.

Gently I roused Thomas. I held him fast in that moment for as long as I could, before his memory also kicked in and he remembered that I was in Paris, or rather, that I should have been in Paris, and began to wonder.

Whispering, I told him what had happened. I sensed his disquiet. If I looked at him his gaze took on a sharpness that I managed to soften slightly if I glanced away as I edged closer and whispered. That nothing had happened. Or hardly anything. It was merely a rift in time. But I was back, we were together, no one had died, no one had been hurt, there had been no tragedies, accidents, disasters, no ambulances or funerals. Even my burn was slowly healing.

Thomas never doubted my story, nor did he need to. I could tell him when the rain would stop and when it would start again, I could tell him that the postman would come by at 10.41 during a light shower, I could describe how soon after that a long-tailed titmouse would flit about the branches of the apple tree, and I could predict that at 5:14 in the afternoon, in the pouring rain, our neighbour would hurry past the fence at the bottom of our back garden, turn right and jog down the path between our house and his own. From the office window we would be able to see him open his gate, cross the paved yard, dodge a puddle that had formed in a hollow where four paving stones met, hurry on up to his back door and unlock it with a key he had ready in his hand, having dug it out of his pocket on his way through the rain.

Those were strange days. We woke in the morning, we went for walks, we sat down and had coffee somewhere on the eighteenth of November. For most of the day as intimately aware of one another as couples in the first flush of love or near-sighted creatures. We made the horizon vanish. We sought this giddy feeling. The distance between us was dispelled in the fog. We made the giddiness a part of our day. Created a bright space out of dazed, grey confusion.

I don't think it was an act of will, but slowly and almost imperceptibly I managed to extend my sense of neutral, indefinite morning. I concentrated it, intensified that pale-grey awakening and with each morning I found it possible to carry that sensation with me further into the day. After only a few mornings I could hold on to the moment long enough for it to encompass everything in the room around me: the bedding and Thomas's body beside me, the wall behind the bed and the wardrobe on the other side of the room, a chair with clothes on it, the morning light, the faint sound of a chimney flue door rattling in the wind. These are familiar sounds and sensations and it is still an ordinary morning, it is spacious and open, and I lie in bed while fragments of the world drift in and dissolve: a brief riff of birdsong, a blackbird defying the grey skies or a robin singing into a pause in the rain, three or four notes to start with, then six or seven, then eight, and each one as it burst forth dissolving in my fog.

It must have been an unconscious exercise in fuzziness, a note on which to start the day. I remember mornings of peace and quiet and soft light. I remember a sort of fog that stayed with us far into the day. We wandered through a misty landscape in which only the outlines of things were discernible. There was no need to know whether the creatures we saw belonged to one species or another, whether the shapes we glimpsed by the road were trees or bushes, whether the buildings we passed were houses or small sheds.

Or we were underwater. We had descended to the bottom of the sea, a couple of divers cautiously exploring our surroundings, pointing out fish or wrecks or forgotten ruins. We communicated through gestures and signs, we singled out certain items for closer examination, picked things up and put them down again. Our explorations had a quiet strangeness to them that we were reluctant to relinquish.

Or maybe we were shipwrecked sailors. Washed up on an un-known shore, surprised and bewildered by our unexpected rescue, astonished to be alive, but with no knowledge of what might await us when we set out to explore the shoreline.

Now, I remember those as the happiest days. Ever. I felt loved. I felt loved on the sofa in the living room and on the floor. I felt loved in bed and when we sat at the dining table in the evening. There was nothing unusual in this. It was no differ-ent from before the eighteenth of November, only stronger, and there was nothing we had to do. This was a time that did not run away with us. It was like the time after we first met, only more intense and possibly – or so it seems to me now – with an undertone of quiet desperation, but that is not how we saw it. There was the feel of electrically charged skin, the way our sentences flowed together when we talked. There was something in the air between us, an intensity, a dense net-work of connections. I felt understood. I uttered sentences that were heard and heard the words that were spoken.

We were living in two different times. That was all. Two times that had flooded their banks. At a place where rivers meet and converge, a kind of temporal Mesopotamia where the Euphrates and the Tigris are merely two different names for water. We were doing fine in Mesopotamia.

We fell into a rhythm. We woke in the morning. I explained my presence. Thomas listened, worried, began to get used to the thought. We went out in the breaks between showers or went for walks by the river in the afternoon. Sometimes, towards the end of the day, Thomas would suddenly see the funny side of the situation and we would fantasise about the consequences of a time which could not hold itself together. We listened to the wind and the rain against the windowpanes, or we went out into the night. At the library in the rue du Vieux Moulin we took out books on parallel universes and multiple worlds. We read tales of pockets, loops and labyrinths in time. We found films about time travel and chronological shifts. We read aloud to one another, we reflected and fantasised and waited for this to make sense of time. We strayed into more fanciful explanations: was it the Roman sestertius, was it love, was it the burn on my hand that had opened the door onto another time? Could there be a natural explanation or were unknown forces at work here?

I don't know if we could be said to have looked for an explanation. We circled. We had no shortage of suggestions, ideas or odd flights of fancy. We went around in a cloud of theories, observations and interpretations. This was something that usually happened late in the afternoon or in the evening, once Thomas had got used to the idea, after we had eaten and were sitting opposite one another at the table in the kitchen, after we had made love and were lying on the floor in the living room or in bed. Our investigation was constantly changing, rather like a dance that led us around the room, an innocent and somewhat clumsy knowledge polka, a wonderment waltz, a blithe ballet of discovery, a hectic tapdance between facts and observations, a questing tango by two dancers who combed the room, never looking for an exit or a place to rest.

We observed things. We heard branches tapping against a windowpane, a plastic plant pot rolling around in the evening breeze, the rain intensifying and letting up, postmen, neighbours and children passing by on the street outside. During the day we shopped and noticed that things might or might not be there the next morning. Sometimes they disappeared during the night. There were inconsistencies, but nothing that we subjected to closer scrutiny. Freshly purchased bread or biscuits vanished overnight only to be found back in the supermarket, where we had bought the last packet on the shelf the day before. Books we had borrowed from the library returned to their shelves in the course of the night. Clothes disappeared: a pair of tights that I never got around to wearing because they weren't there the next morning. There were repetitions and anomalies. We observed, we wondered, but never for long and I don't think we really wanted to find an explanation. We were prepared to accept any theory that described our situation with only reasonable accuracy and ready to drop it again if we came up with another.

We found patterns but didn't investigate them more closely. We found inconsistencies; we wondered about them and then forgot them. I remember this as a shared thing, but they were my patterns, it was my wondering, because come the morning Thomas would have forgotten everything we had unearthed and our day would start all over again. We made minor discoveries and found quick explanations. We didn't amass knowledge because everything we discovered I retained very loosely in my memory, it was all easy to shake off in mutual forgetfulness and just as easy to recall when the question arose again.

Often, we would simply come to the conclusion that you cannot know everything, that you have to accept some displacement in life, that you have to expect inconsistencies, and that was what we encountered: patterns and inconsistencies, two worlds trying to merge.

This went on for some weeks. Or for a number of days corresponding to several weeks. Sixty-three days, perhaps. Sixty-four. Or sixty-five. I don't know. I don't really remember when it began to go the other way.

I had counted the days, but each day was just a stroke in a small notebook which I kept in the kitchen. At the beginning, this was something we talked about: the number of days and of strokes in my notebook, but it was soon consigned to a drawer in the little table in the kitchen. During the day I would find a moment when I was alone to open the drawer, take out the notebook, make a stroke in it, close it again and slip it back into the drawer. The number of days was no longer something we talked about. We couldn't let the days come between us: I kept the distance shut away in a drawer in the kitchen.

After a while, though, clarity returned. It became harder to hold on. The fog lifted. Or the divers resurfaced. The ship-wrecked sailors became familiar with the shoreline. The days became more clearly defined. Not the first moments. My morning started in the same way as before. I became aware of the room around me, a day unfolding; I could still hold on to the feeling of a grey, misty morning for a few notes of birdsong, four or five notes, later only three, maybe two, no more, then my moment splintered and I remembered every-thing, my thoughts were already scanning the room, they had drifted to the windowsill, out into the morning, to the birds in the tree, to houses and streets where, one after another, people were entering the eighteenth of November in a firmly established pattern, convinced that they were embarking on this day for the very first time.

My morning acquired depth and a clear horizon. I didn't want a horizon, though. I wanted grey morning light and a day that began with no time, no memory and no plans, but that was no longer possible. A few notes from a bird in No-vember, a sharply defined room and a day that could not be held back. There was a clarity to the air and instead of a vague awareness of the bedding, the room and the soft morning light, these things were now the elements of the eighteenth of

November, the day's sharp-edged props. Thomas, lying next to me, was no longer my sleeping husband on some indeterminate morning, but my husband moving away, day by day, my not yet lost love, whose look of surprise I was about to meet, because this was no ordinary morning and I was no longer Tara, half-asleep, nebulously alive and quietly happy, but Tara back in a broken time and yet again I had to explain to Thomas what had happened. I would see his disquiet and hasten to say that he didn't have to worry, that I was here, that we were together, no one had died, no one had been hurt. I was home, I was all right, we were alive; it was only time that had fallen apart.

I had lost my morning fog. The day stood out in sharp relief, in colour and fully clothed – sometimes from the moment that I awoke, sometimes after a few seconds – but there was no longer anything I could do to put it off. The day had become the eighteenth of November # 68, # 69, # 70, # 71.

Eventually the clarity became too much. There were no mitigating circumstances. I tried to tell Thomas what had happened, but my explanations sounded hazy, inadequate. I tried saying that no one was dead or hurt. That my burn had healed and that there was only a little red scar left. That he didn't need to worry. But a note of unease had crept into my own voice. I was beginning to see more keenly, I had started to look for explanations, and there was no fog now in which to hide. I felt unprotected. I felt alone.

That was when I came in here. It was one of those mornings when I had woken up knowing instantly all that had happened. I woke to the familiar room, to the same grey light, the soft morning rain, the birds outside, their autumn voices and brief sequences of notes, so well known to me, but all of it presented itself without the protective filter of sleep. It must have been day # 76, because I put my daily stroke in the notebook with a pen that I found on the table in here, in the guest room, in the room overlooking the garden, the apple tree and a woodpile.

Seventy-six days was too many. The distance was too great. I stood in the kitchen with the notebook in my hand and knew that too many days had come between us. I looked for the pencil that usually lay in the drawer with the notebook, but it wasn't there. I stared at the long line of strokes in the book and suddenly it seemed impossible for me to locate another pencil, make yet another stroke, put the notebook back in the drawer, wake Thomas and tell him that I was back, that no one was injured or dead, it was merely that some days had come between us. I couldn't carry on with our repetitions. The fog had lifted, the landscape stretched out clear and sharp before me and we were not waking to the same day.

I picked up all traces of myself. I collected my books and clothes from the bedroom and tiptoed down the stairs. As quietly as I could I cleared up in the kitchen, fetched an empty plastic bottle that had been in my bag since I got home, rinsed it and slowly filled it with water from the tap. Then I gathered all my books together and put them in my bag, took the notebook containing all of my strokes from the kitchen table and slipped the bag over my shoulder. All was quiet in the house as I crept softly along the hall to fetch my coat and my boots, opened the door of the guest room, slipped in here and closed the door behind me.

I lay on the bed for five days. I don't know what was happening, but I think of it as one long, grinding round of questions going on in a brain that had expended all its energy on holding on to that morning vagueness, a blissful haze. I recall what was going on in my mind as a kind of crazed, intuitive rationality, aimless and incessant, a wild mental race through details and patterns, a never-ending review of technical data, an enumeration of facts, an intense accumulation of events and a résumé of incidents from all the days I had spent in the eighteenth of November.

All of the things that Thomas and I might have considered, all the reflections that we had allowed to melt into the fog, now came rolling and tumbling over me, throwing me into a sort of rational delirium. The questioning that I had been warding off now set in all unbidden, dredging up data from the days I had spent with Thomas.

I already knew the day outside the house, with its weather and its events. From my memory I drew information on the coming and going of people on the streets, I remembered the movements of the birds, the sound of the wind in the trees, the rain tailing off and intensifying, the sound of a plastic plant pot being blown around the cobbles at the corner of the house.

Now new details were added. While my memory was working at top speed my brain was harvesting the sounds from a succession of absolutely identical days: a person moving around the house, footsteps over the floors and on the stairs, drawers being opened, the rustle of carrier bags, a hand or an arm brushing a wall, the gush of water through pipes, doors being opened and closed. It was a collection of movements, an accumulation of details, of the day's patterns, and all of it folded into an incessant questioning, a logical grinding, a cool fever, free-ranging brain activity, organising and rationalising without any help from me, rather like data processing, conducted without any human interference. There were parts of the brain which were constantly at work – as if construction processes were under way: an operation which was almost painful, which sliced up the day, drew information from the cut surfaces and put them back together to form a new pattern, a new universe.

At times, I was overcome by an almost total exhaustion that would suddenly wash over me and plunge me straight into a deep sleep which I would wake from, seemingly without having dreamt, and which segued seamlessly into the incessant collecting and processing of information.

I don't know what was happening. I put the day together. I rebuilt the day. Perhaps I was preparing for another time. Perhaps it was a case of neural reprogramming, a calibration of the mental instruments, the formation of new synapses between the brain cells, the creation of receptors, the production of neurotransmitters, maybe a rearrangement of my sense of time, an extension to the brain or the demolition of buildings that had outlived their use, what do I know? I know that it felt as though I were a building site, an anthill, a beehive, a laboratory full of activity. I know that now and then I drank or ate, not much, but I had found a couple of packets of biscuits and two tins of apricots in syrup, left by Thomas's grandfather. I must have taken them from one of the kitchen cabinets during the night or while Thomas was out, I don't remember, but I do remember that I would sometimes go through to the kitchen to fill a plastic bottle with water. I also remember that I occasionally climbed out of the window and peed behind the garden shed, and I have the idea that I sometimes wandered around the house when Thomas was out, but that memory is unclear so I can't be certain. What I remember best from those days is the interminable grinding, as if the days I had been through since the first eighteenth of November were now being condensed, as if all information was being pooled and stored in my memory. In went all the days we had spent together. In went all the days which, one after another, Thomas lost at night, all the days I had tried to shake off along the way, but they had all, nonetheless, stuck in my mind.

The fog had lifted. Those strange days were past. I knew I couldn't hold on to the morning's hazy grey light for long, that I had been keeping the past and the present out, that I had been like a human pilot light. Gone were the featureless mornings. Gone, my time at the bottom of the sea, gone and irretrievable. Gone, the fog which had been the greatest bliss but which – it seems to me now – requires one to be in a state of the utmost naivety, to dwell in the halls of folly, to surrender to the gentle grip of apathy.

For five days I lay on the spare bed in here. Then I went back. It was day 81. I could see that five strokes had been made with a pen in my notebook and I vaguely remember standing at the table, almost mechanically making a mark in the book. I have the impression that I did this every morning after Thomas went out, but I'm not sure. Sitting at the desk in this room I now counted all the strokes and instead of adding yet another, I wrote # 81 with the pen. As if I craved precision. As if I needed to count the days, one by one. They had to be numbered, I could not make do with strokes in a notebook.

That morning I had woken already immersed in the by now familiar brain activity, but then words started to come into my mind. Phrases like 'rational delirium' and 'logical grind' emerged from the constant buzzing in my head.

Later I began to notice the room around me. I became aware

that I was lying on the bed and that I could hear the rain on the windows. Then I caught a faint whiff of sweat, unbrushed teeth and unwashed clothes. I remember glancing around for a moment before realising that it came from me. I also remember feeling cold and thinking to myself: here lies Tara Selter, feeling cold. 'Morning chill,' I thought. Not long afterwards I heard Thomas on the stairs and told myself that at least I knew this much: there was no variation. I knew when he would turn on the tap, fill the kettle and put it on the stove.

I went out there in the afternoon, after Thomas had gone out. I heard music in the living room, I heard him pick up the parcels from the hall floor and I heard him leave the house. I was a different person. The turmoil in my head had stilled, I was hungry and I needed a bath. I went upstairs, took a bath, went down to the kitchen, cut myself a slice of bread and ate it. In the vegetable drawer I found a pear that must have been in the fridge since my first foggy days, sliced it in half, then into quarters and ate the pieces one by one. Then I sat down in the living room and waited for Thomas. I knew his day. I knew he would be back once the rain set in, but I was still not sure of the exact time.

Not long after the rain started in earnest I saw our neighbour walking past the fence and moments later Thomas came into view, drenched and without an umbrella. I hurried out into the hall, switched on the light and opened the door.

He stared at me in surprise. We met in the doorway. I helped him off with his soaking wet coat and told him that I was back. I fetched a sweater from the bedroom, made a cup of tea and led him into the living room, where we sat down: all of this while I told him about Paris and Philip Maurel and Marie, about the missing books and the sestertius. I told him about our strange hazy days. I described the lifting of the fog and the clear-cut mornings with definite horizons. I told him about the strokes in my notebook and my spell in the guest room. I told him that I was a different person. That something had happened to my head. I led him to the guest room. My smell still hung in the air in here. There were packets of biscuits on the floor and a couple of empty apricot tins. I said that I needed his help. I showed him the notebook with the long line of strokes in pencil, then five made with a pen and, below them: # 81. I told him that I had to make sense of time. I had to know how time worked. I told him about the logical grind, the construction site of rationality, the brain's development work, the harvesting of sounds, the mental data processing. I told him that I had to find the rift in time, that I had to know how I had slipped through it and how to return to progressive time. I said I thought he could help.

I could tell that he believed me. I was different. A path seemed to have been swept in my head, slabs laid, a patch of scrub cleared, a road built, snow shovelled, whatever, but I had to move on. I had to find some answers. I had to find an explanation and a way out. I was starting to believe that if only I could figure out the mechanisms I could get the day to resume its familiar progressive course.

For twenty-seven days we investigated the mechanics of the day. In the morning I woke to clarity, to a day with a foreground, a middle ground and a distant but distinct horizon. Lying in bed next to Thomas, even before I opened my eyes I knew what had happened. I got out of bed and went downstairs to assemble my observations and findings from the previous day. I woke Thomas and explained everything to him. I summed up our investigations and presented the main conclusions. He had to help. There was no fog to get lost in. I insisted on asking questions. How had the damage occurred? Could such an event be explained or was it pure chance, an accident? Where was the rift in time? What had I done on the day when time fell apart? Was someone to blame? Had someone made a mistake, and if so what?

But the seventeenth of November had been an uneventful day. I had travelled to Bordeaux. I had bought books and gone on to Paris. The eighteenth of November had been an uneventful day. I had woken in the morning, I had had breakfast, I had read a newspaper, I had seen a piece of bread fall to the floor, had bought some books and taken two of them away with me in my bag. I had called on a friend, or possibly two friends, had burned my hand, spoken on the phone, slept with ice cubes.

We could not find the mistake. We could not find the reason why time had fallen apart. There was no reason. I could not find a reason, Thomas could not find a reason. We could find patterns and we could find inconsistencies. Thomas was the pattern, I was disturbance.

It had been plain from the very first day that my body followed me. The burn from Philip's shop had adhered to my hand, it had stayed with me as a small swollen and painful wound, it wept, it formed a scab which eventually fell off, leaving a red scar which gradually, day by day, had contracted and grown smaller. I did not wake up with a hand unscathed by the eighteenth of November. The wound had done exactly what one would expect of such a burn, moving through time and changing a little each day. Time acted on my skin and now, when I looked in the bathroom mirror, my eye was also caught by my hair. It was longer. I hadn't noticed it before, but now I could see that my hair had grown, not much, but enough to leave me in no doubt. My face in the mirror looked the same and if there were any changes they were so slight as to be imperceptible, but my hair had grown as the days had passed.

It was not so surprising: one day followed another, the burn healed, hair grew and my body kept pace, as if nothing had happened. My nails had grown long, I had a vague memory of standing in the bathroom with nail clippers in my hand, but of those first foggy days my recollection was grey and hazy.

Now, though, it was obvious, so I cut my nails, or rather, I cut them again, slowly, over the sink in the bathroom, because they had grown, as if time existed and I was snipping tiny slivers of time into the sink, then I turned on the tap and washed them down the drain.

But Thomas was his old self. There was no change there. Our days together had been different, but none of them stuck in his mind or his body. They vanished overnight, passed through him, leaving no trace, and each morning he woke up exactly the same as before. We were living in two different times, our bodies were living in two different times. Not just our memories. Our bodies too.

The things around us were less predictable. The books I had bought at the auction in Bordeaux on the seventeenth of November had stayed on the table in my hotel room, exactly where I had left them, but *Histoire des Eaux Potables* and Thornton's *Heavenly Bodies*, which I had purchased on the eighteenth, remained a mystery. It was hard to see why, in the first instance, they had returned to the antiquarian bookshops where I had bought them, why only the next day they had stayed with me, safe under my pillow, and why, after several days, they stayed wherever I left them without any problem. I had carried them around with me, afraid that they would disappear, but they were soon sitting on the table in the living room as if they belonged there, as if they had been trained to stay put.

It was the inconsistencies that puzzled us. A lot of things had gone back to their original locations. The heater and the blue gas cylinder had returned to the back room in Philip Maurel's shop. Even the dust had been back in place. The Roman sestertius had disappeared. I had searched for it and I am sure that it is now lying in its box on the counter in Philip Maurel's shop. But if the sestertius had gone back to where it had come from why hadn't my bag, my clothes and all the other things I had taken to Paris not returned to the hotel room, where they had been on the first eighteenth of November? They had stayed with me in the house and every morning they were exactly where I had left them the day before. On my first evening home my bag had been sitting on the living-room floor, later in a corner of the bedroom and now it is here next to me, propped against the wall, and the books are on the little table by the bed. As if, in the midst of all the unpredictability I can carry them with me, draw them into my time and make them stay there.

We could discern no clear pattern and this bothered me. I wanted to find a pattern and break it, but instead we discovered too many unknowns for us to comprehend the mechanics of the day. There were grey areas and unanswered questions.

Obviously I added each day to the collection of eighteenths of November we went through and remembered them all, and just as obviously everyone else had forgotten them by the time they opened their eyes the next morning. I no longer remember the individual days very clearly though, they are shrouded in mist and run together in my memory, but they have not disappeared.

I remember that we left traces. Things were affected. We consumed things. First we had trouble finding the coffee we usually bought. It was sold out, so we bought another brand, but it was us who had drunk the coffee from the shelf in the little supermarket in the rue Clémentine Giroux. Likewise, it was us who had emptied the shelf of orange-flavoured chocolate. We had noticed that the shelf was empty and I remember finding this odd, but we bought other kinds of chocolate instead, we bought the pure dark chocolate, we bought the peppermint or caramel-flavoured ones.

Sometimes things returned to their starting point. We had bought the last jar of olives on the supermarket shelf, we had put it in the kitchen cabinet and the next day it had disappeared from the house but was once more to be found in the shop. I think we bought it again, opened it and had some olives with lunch and I think the half-empty jar was still in the fridge the following day, but I'm not sure, because during our foggy days this was not something we checked.

Nor had we checked our bank account, which now proved to have gone back to square one every day. Each morning the balance was the same and even though several of our purchases showed up in the account in the evening, the next morning they were gone. On the very first morning we had also noticed that there was no sign on Thomas's phone of our calls to one another. I remembered that I had already been having problems with my mobile on the train to Clairon and before long it had gone completely dead, but I hadn't needed a phone so it wasn't something we dwelt on. We had had other things to think about. We had foggy mornings and rainy days, we had more important things to see to and when the day's inconsistencies cropped up in our conversations we quickly changed the subject.

But I no longer wanted to change the subject. I wanted to know. I wanted answers. Thomas hesitated. I insisted. We bought things and left them lying in the kitchen. We opened them or left them unopened. We observed and we kept notes. Usually, the items that we hadn't opened disappeared during the night and went back to where we had bought them. We took things up to the bedroom with us at night, I bought a jar of olives and placed it on the windowsill, I put a toothbrush, unopened and still in its box, under my pillow. The following morning the toothbrush was still there, box and all, but the jar of olives was gone and a packet of tea which Thomas had put in a kitchen cabinet had also vanished.

It was clear that the day always returned to its starting point, but that there were also variations. It was not mechanical, there was more to it. It was the same day which kept recurring, but it was not set in stone. I remembered. Thomas forgot. I moved through time. Thomas stayed still. Objects followed different patterns. It was not simple – it was almost as if the things themselves were in doubt, as if they hesitated, as if they wavered between the different possibilities offered by time, teetering on the line between time that passed and time that rewound.

We searched for the point at which the day rewound, but there was no one point. It didn't happen at midnight. It might have happened in the early hours, but we couldn't pin it down: the magic moment when everything went back. It was not when the clock struck midnight, it was not at ten past two and it was not at 4:35 in the morning. There was no precision, there were no rules.

Every morning I woke Thomas and explained what had happened. I told him that he had to help me. That I had slipped into another time. Maybe my brain had been rearranged, I said. I needed help. I could not think the whole thing through by myself. We had to find an explanation. He had to think too.

On one of the first nights after I re-emerged from this room we stayed awake all night and Thomas managed to follow me into the next morning. At midnight nothing happened. Thomas stuck with me. He remembered our day, he remembered that it was the night after the eighteenth of November, not the night before the eighteenth.

One o'clock came and nothing happened. Two o'clock and nothing happened. By three o'clock we were growing tired, but we had promised each other that we would stay awake. We had coffee and made love. We went through to the kitchen and made something to eat. We read aloud to one another and took a bath together. If we went from one room to another we did so together. We talked to one another on the way downstairs, we held hands on the way up. Neither of us let the other one out of their sight. We stayed focused, we moved in step and did everything as one. We were Siamese twins, a team of horses, two lumberjacks sawing through a tree trunk. We wanted to cross into the next eighteenth of November together, we wanted to leave the eighteenth of November together. I had all my attention trained on Thomas and he had no chance to forget that I was there with him in the house.

A little after five o'clock he must, however, have lost concentration for a moment, or maybe I wasn't paying attention, because suddenly he thought he had been asleep. We were lying on the floor in the living room, on the black-and-white rug. He had rolled over for a moment while I was still stroking his back and all at once he gave a start, his body jerking the way it sometimes does just as you're falling asleep, but I don't think he was sleeping, because he had been in the middle of a sentence and he was finishing it as he turned over. He gazed at me, looking a little confused, like a sleepwalker who has been abruptly wakened.

He asked what time it was, what day it was, what had we been drinking, because he didn't feel very well. Not long afterwards he asked when I had got back, because he had forgotten me coming home. Had I got back earlier than expected, had I arrived during the night and how had my trip home been?

No shred of recollection remained. No bath or coffee in the middle of the night, no sleepy talks or nocturnal meals could be dredged up from his memory. There were no twins, no team of horses or lumberjacks. There was a distance between us. There was a hole in time, but there was no way of telling how it had happened. A moment's inattention and Thomas had lost his eighteenth of November. His memory had been wiped clean again, not by a long night's slumber, there had been no gradual dissipation. It was as if his eighteenth of November had fallen through a crack in the night, a chasm that had suddenly opened up. But we could not see how it had happened, we could not find the fault in time and we could not come up with an explanation.

Yet again I told him the whole story. I explained that time had fallen apart, that we were investigating the problem from within, that we had examined it in great detail, that we could no longer hide in a foggy day, that he had to help me, that there were no dead or injured, only a time fraught with riddles, with inconsistencies, an unpredictable mechanism, a blurred equation with far too many unknowns.

We fell asleep in the living room and woke up late. Thomas woke first and he remembered everything I had told him in the early hours, but our day together, our evening and our nocturnal investigations, all of that was gone. All he remembered was what I had told him: that time had fallen apart, that he had to help me, and he was already considering the situation when I woke.

We spent the afternoon together. We went out to do the shopping, we went back to the house, we discussed the particulars of time and I insisted on trying, once more, to find the fault in time.

That same night we stayed awake again. With our wits sharpened, refreshed after our long sleep that day. We noted down observations and homed in on the slightest thing. Late in the night we fried eggs and sat down across from one another at the kitchen table. We commented on every detail of what was happening, to ensure that we were both focusing on the same thing. I held on to the frying pan with one hand and kept my eyes fixed on Thomas while he poured oil into the pan and got eggs out of the fridge. He cracked the eggs and slid them into the pan, first one, then another, while I watched his hands. We remarked on a piece of eggshell floating in the translucent egg white which I carefully fished out; on the tiny bubbles in the oil around the edge of the frying egg; on the glistening membrane covering the yolk, on the heat distribution, on whiteness and translucence, on the moment when the whiteness reaches the edge of the yolk, on the sprinkling of pepper, of salt. We talked about the surprise of childhood eggs with double yolks: there you were, in the kitchen with your mother or your grandfather, you cracked an egg and, if it was a particularly large egg, often there would be two yolks in the bowl. We talked about keeping chickens, our garden was big enough, there was space for a henhouse at the bottom of the vegetable plot. We got out plates and cutlery, talking as we did so about the sound of plates and cutlery, the sound of china and of metal. I took the pan off the gas while Thomas put out a table mat, I set the pan with the fried eggs on the table, we sat down across from one another and ate.

We collected details. We stayed alert. We kept our eyes fixed on each other. On the table. On the empty pan between us. For ten minutes or more we simply sat there at the table. We talked about the objects around us. We speculated as to whether things disappeared in fits and starts or all at once. Thomas believed there would be things in other rooms in the house that had already returned to their places. We talked about going to check but didn't get up. We talked about cameras which could record changes. We talked about love. About whether it could make things happen. About whether love could bring us in or out.

And then, from one moment to the next, the frying pan was gone. I froze for a second and glanced around the kitchen, but the pan was nowhere to be seen. I got up and as I did so I heard Thomas cry out. He wanted to know what had happened. He was troubled. He wasn't drowsy or tired. He was simply troubled. He could not remember what he was doing in the kitchen. He had gone to bed on the night of the seventeenth, only hours after we had spoken on the phone. Now here he was in the kitchen. I was supposed to be in Paris. But here I was, looking for a frying pan.

I forgot about the frying pan and sat down again across from Thomas. I explained what had happened and saw anxiety course through him as I led him down the long road from my first eighteenth of November to the fried eggs we had just eaten. But he didn't feel as if he had recently eaten a fried egg. In fact he was now feeling a little peckish. I showed him the carton in the fridge containing not six, but four eggs. I showed him a receipt, dated November 18th, detailing the purchase of six eggs, I showed him the time stamp. But there were no eggshells in the rubbish bag. The eggshells had disappeared, but the cast-iron hob on which he had fried the eggs was still slightly warm, and the grocery receipt, which had been in my bag, had not gone anywhere. There were inconsistencies in time and it was impossible to discern a pattern that made sense.

For the first time I found it frightening. Not merely bewildering and odd and a little bit sinister. It was frightening, it was senseless and in no way magical. The fog had cleared completely. This was not the feeling of unease from the moment of the falling slice of bread at the hotel, nor was it the sense of a grey area between us. We were not wanderers through misty landscapes, we were not divers or shipwrecked sailors. We were not twins or a team of horses, we were not lumberjacks or double yolks in an egg. Had we been in Mesopotamia the rivers would have acquired names and flowed back into their normal courses. The sky would be clear, the sun blazing down, the rivers would have dried up, troop formations would be discernible, stark silhouettes would patrol the banks, the clink of steel would be heard. We were living in two different times and there was no hiding the differences. Two territories that bounded on one another, with frontier feuds and obscure inter-zone transactions. We were lovers in a combat zone. Thomas had no recollection of our days together, we could not create foggy days, floods and hazy mornings, we could not find a way forward together, we were in no way double or misty or parallel. I could find no clarity or patterns, and no way out.

Again we tried in vain to get the fault in time to make sense, again we went to bed and again Thomas could remember our early-morning conversation but nothing else. He remembered his confusion in the kitchen, he remembered my account of events, my lengthy explanations, my detailed description of our investigations, but his own memories of our evening and night had yet again been erased, wiped away, they'd slipped through a crack in the night.

The next few days were all alike. I woke with a start, immediately remembering all that had happened. I sat up in bed and looked at Thomas sleeping peacefully beside me. I got up and went down to the living room. I made plans for the day. I assembled the observations from the previous day and compared them with those of the other days. I drew up diagrams and tables. I made graphs and lists. I stuck notes on the living-room wall and highlighted the day's problems in red or green.

Then I woke Thomas. I told him what had happened. I sensed his disquiet. He hesitated. I insisted, and we investigated the day. In the course of the morning he was presented with the main observations and results of our previous investigations. I showed him sketches illustrating time's patterns and tables outlining the days' facts. During the day we discussed possible explanations, we drew graphs and set up systems, we created columns and wrote summaries, but the next morning, when Thomas woke once more to his first eighteenth of November, he had forgotten everything and once more I had to tell him what had happened and how far we had got with our investigations.

The living room had become a control room. The wall provided the background for notes and graphs. The black-and-white rug became the venue for briefings and recaps. The armchairs by the window were our staff-room where we would take brief breaks from our labours. During the day we noted down observations and facts, in the evening we reviewed the day's deliberations. We outlined details and variations. We came up with rules and exceptions to them. We underlined and crossed out. But our investigations bore no fruit. Or rather: they bore plenty of fruit, masses of observations, details which explained nothing and explanations which didn't quite fit.

We were living in two different times, that was a fact. At the start of the day, I was the only one who knew this, that too was a fact. Not until after the morning report, after a short briefing over breakfast and after a comprehensive review of the lists, diagrams and graphs in the living room, did Thomas understand what I was asking him to take part in. It was also a fact that the boundaries were fluid. That there was no specific point at which the shift occurred. We could journey some way into the night together, but sooner or later time fell out of joint. It was a fact that the objects of the world sometimes stayed with me and sometimes went back to where they had come from. That the way things behaved seemed to be unpredictable. That it helped to keep them physically close, but that there was something unpredictable about the workings of time.

We focused. We devised theories and frameworks which we compared to the events of the eighteenth of November. We debated perceptions of reality and mental dysfunctions, we considered whether I might be generating trains of fictional experiences or whether everyone else had been struck by some form of amnesia, or whether we had stepped into a wave of psychological incongruence. We propounded theories and mounted counter-arguments. We read about parataxic views of time and variable chronometry, we unearthed descriptions of fractures in time and chronotoxic recurrence. We explored theories on parallel universes, multiple worlds and relative temporal structures. We found stories of the morphology of memory and of rare cases of amnesiac chronopathy. We discussed theories of repetition and mnemonic defects. We studied mental processes, the objects of the world, temporal sequences. We collected theories and explanations.

Actually, though, we had no shortage of explanations, we had plenty of those, but explanations which could stand up to critical scrutiny and at the same time embody all our many observations, those we could not find. All our lines of enquiry came to dead ends, we explored each strand thoroughly and returned empty-handed every time. There were flaws and a lack of coherence, there were facts that didn't fit, there were contradictions and paradoxes. Every system fell apart the minute we tried to put all our data together to form a whole. There was no consistency, we could not get the facts of the day to square with certain of our theories, we could not construct coherent systems or find any pattern, and all our detailed explanations had to be rejected one after the other. Every time we came to a dead end we had to go back to the facts: Thomas was subject to the laws of forgetfulness, and I was accumulating too many days in my memory. Thomas was caught in eternity and I was slowly but surely moving towards my grave.

With each day that passed, my hope that everything would suddenly return to normal grew fainter and even though sometimes in the morning and well into the forenoon Thomas believed that the damage was only fleeting, by the evening, after a long day's deliberations he too had usually lost faith in the idea of any return to normality. There weren't many traces left of our foggy days, there was no smooth passage through the eighteenth of November, the jokes about the unpredictability of time had all but dried up, as had those early hours when we would lie and listen to the night and I would provide a running commentary on all the sounds it produced while Thomas lay there giggling in the dark at my ability to predict the exact order of a series of nocturnal noises.

Now the fun was over and all that remained were the pointless investigations that filled our day: our vain attempts to fathom the mystery of time; the countless questions we had to give up answering, again and again, and usually – often around the point when we were in the kitchen, making dinner – we gave up on our explanations and turned to the question of what was to become of us. Would we be able to stick together? Would I be able to face Thomas each morning and tell him about more and more days, fresh explanations, collapsing houses of cards, dead ends and narrow passages?

And yet, in the midst of all this I remember sudden glimpses of hope, little hints of change, the thought that one day we would wake up to the nineteenth of November, or that all at once we would break through to a day in January or February. Sooner or later time must surely always revert to its eternal forward progression, as Thomas said on the first evening, and sometimes, out of the blue, one of us would repeat his words, not ironically or bitterly, not dolefully or with disappointment in our voices, but with hope, with perfectly ordinary and easily recognisable hope. Occasionally we would run into a small fog bank: moments reminiscent of our first days, and sometimes we had the feeling that we understood this time, that we could get to the bottom of the problem and were close to finding a solution. But deep down I knew that we were trapped down a dead end. There was no way back to those foggy days and no explanations to be found, no matter how many observations we noted down or systems we devised.

I stayed with Thomas for twenty-seven days. Then I realised that I would have to investigate the matter by myself. For the first time in our life together I had to make plans on my own. I did not yet know what had to be done, but I knew I could not go on, morning after morning, recounting a longer and longer succession of variations on the same day. We could not share the eighteenth of November. This was a day I had to carry alone.

That same evening, while Thomas was brushing his teeth, I packed my bag. While he was getting undressed I dismantled the control room, gathered our tables and notes into a pile which I put into a brown cardboard box, and while he was in the bathroom I quickly carried my bag and the box of papers in here. I tidied up, so the kitchen looked like the one that Thomas had woken to on his first eighteenth of November. I had picked a couple of apples from the tree in the garden and these I put in a bowl on the kitchen table. I poured half of the loose tea from the bag in the kitchen cabinet into an empty tin which I hid behind some bags of flour and I emptied the fridge of our purchases from the eighteenth of November.

The next morning I moved in here. It was day 108. I was awake before it was light and lay for a long time listening to Thomas, asleep in the morning gloom, before slipping softly out of bed, folding the duvet back behind me and smoothing it out so it didn't look as if it had been used. I picked up my clothes and crept down the stairs. Very gently I opened the door of this room, laid my clothes on a chair, collected the pile of books from the living room and picked up a couple of drawing pins and a red felt-tip pen that had fallen on the floor in there. I fetched a cup, a plate and some cutlery from the kitchen and set them on the table in here. I got my coat and boots from the hall, brought them in here as well and shut the door. Soon there was no trace of me left in the rest of the house apart from a little warmth under the duvet in the bedroom, a minor difference in temperature which would slowly disappear, and by the time Thomas woke that warmth would be gone and my visit to his eighteenth of November would be forgotten.

A few hours later, waking in the spare bed, I could hear Thomas's footsteps on the stairs. He had woken to forgetfulness and an ordinary eighteenth of November. While I, in the guest room, had woken to my eighteenth of November # 108.

124

Last night was a late one. I switched off the light before Thomas went upstairs, but I did not go to sleep. I lay on the bed and waited and when I was sure he would be asleep I got up, went over to the table and sat down, switched on my lamp and carried on writing. I have written the eighteenth of November again and again and still the nineteenth hasn't come. I can hear it in the day. I have woken to the same sounds and the same day. It is a pattern I know. It is the pattern of the eighteenth of November and I am getting used to that thought.

The air around me is still chilly, but Thomas has lit a fire in the living room and I catch the faint whiff of smoke wafting under the door. It is the downdraught that does it: the wind direction or a sudden gust of wind blowing smoke back down the chimney, but that will soon clear. I have eaten some dry bread which was meant for the birds and now there is none left for them, but in the afternoon when Thomas puts on the music in the living room I'll leave the house and go down to the supermarket in the rue Clémentine Giroux and buy bread for the birds, then I'll hurry home again and Thomas will be out and the birds will be fed, the blackbirds and the robin, the titmice – great and long-tailed – and all. I will buy birdseed and bread, I will buy suet balls and whatever else is on offer for hungry birds, because I have eaten their bread and they need to be fed, and once they've been fed I will probably have a bath, I might make an omelette, I must remember to buy eggs, maybe I should get a hotplate, it could sit in the corner. Maybe there's healing in sentences. It is day 124. Tomorrow I will write # 125 and the day after tomorrow I will write # 126, and there is nothing to be done about it.

I am conscious of my mood today. It fluctuates. I am a little grumpy this morning, I can tell, but that's probably due to lack of sleep. I look around the room and smile at my mess. My boots are in the middle of the floor; there are clothes and papers scattered about, a couple of plates and some dirty cups on the table, a pencil on the floor under my chair, shavings on the table from last night's sharpened pencils. I'm tired, but I'm also aware of a faint sense of satisfaction, like the feeling you get when you wake up to a mess of your own making but know that there's no mistake. There is a reason for the mess. There was important work to be done.

The place is a mess because I spent the night remembering. Because I dwell in the eighteenth of November. It is late afternoon and Thomas must have been out while I was asleep.

I didn't hear him go out or come back and I am sitting at a table with a pile of paper in front of me on which I have written that it is the eighteenth of November and that my name is Tara Selter. I feel as if I am no longer alone. As if someone is listening. My days have not been lost to oblivion. They exist. My days exist in my pile of paper, they have not been erased during the night, the paper remembers and on it I can see that it says day number this and day number that and the eighteenth of November but never the nineteenth.

I have written down everything I remember about days that keep repeating themselves, everything I know about the eighteenth of November. But now I don't know any more. I moved in here on day 108 and since then nothing has happened. I have woken up in the morning, I have looked out at the rain and the birds in the garden, I have listened to the sounds in the house and in the afternoon, once I could hear the strains of music issuing from the living room, I have gone out. Then one day I started to write: that it was the eighteenth of November and that there was someone in the house. That is still the situation. I have reached this point and there is nothing more to tell. All I have to show for days and days of trying to remember my long succession of days is a pile of paper and a messy room.

And now I have no more to say. About anything. Or rather. I have no more to say about Tara Selter. I don't know what is happening. I cannot tell the future. But I think this will go on. And on. I think that this day will be like all the other days and once this day is over there will be a new eighteenth of November and so it will continue, day after day, and if one day I write # 365 a year will have passed and then it will be the eighteenth of November again, and what then?

I don't know. I know this day. I can say what the weather will be like in a moment. I can say how the day will go in the house, I can tell of birds and rainclouds, I can say which greengrocers will have their stalls set up at the market on the place Mignolet in the afternoon, I can tell who will be in the queue at the supermarket in the rue Clémentine Giroux shortly before half-past three and who will come down the steps at the Café La Petite Èchelle at ten to five, but I can say nothing about my own future. All I can say is that I woke up in the room overlooking the garden and a woodpile and I have woken up in a very different mood. I have actually woken in a mood. I have a mood. That is new.

129

So something has happened after all. Tara Selter, alone in the eighteenth of November, has acquired a mood. It comes over me almost every day, not for the whole day, but suddenly it is there, it is noticeable. Today is no exception, I am a mite irritable, maybe it's boredom, but it makes me happy, because there is open space around me and there is room for a mood. It feels almost as if there is someone living in here. A fluctuating mood is rather like a dance, it really swings, even though there isn't much room. There is room enough in here for my mood to shift. Now it shifts again. Gaiety fills the room.

136

I am not saying I have lost hope. It just doesn't come by so often any more. It has moved away. It was quite undramatic, it did not slam the door behind it, it is more as if, like an animal, it has found new hunting grounds, like a cat that has moved next door or a plant that has scattered its seeds where they are more likely to grow.

But instead I have acquired a mood. It is not the same as hope, but it is not nothing. I have also acquired an electric kettle and a hotplate, which I bought in the ironmonger's in town. I bought a frying pan as well. I have exchanged my hope for a mood and a frying pan.

Often I feel my mood rising to the surface as soon as I wake, but I seldom feel hope. I don't wake up in the morning and think that this might be the day. That I might have woken to the nineteenth or to another kind of morning, to December or January, for example. To February frost or a day in March. I do not go to the window hoping that the weather has changed and it's a long time since I went to bed thinking that maybe, when I woke up, the day would be different.

I am not saying I have lost hope, I am simply saying that it seldom comes to call. I cannot sit down and wait, safe in the knowledge that it will turn up, I cannot summon it to me, but sometimes, nonetheless, hope comes back. Unexpectedly, out of the blue. Like last night.

It happened because I had gone out into the garden. Because it was the middle of the night, because I needed to pee, because I opened the door into the hall and crept out of the back door. It was cold, I walked barefoot across the lawn, past the apple tree and over to the hedge. The sky was clouded over, I peed in the darkness and then got up, meaning to go straight back to the house, but at that moment the clouds broke just at the spot where the moon had been hanging hidden.

There was nothing odd about that. Thomas and I have been out in the garden at night several times and occasionally we have seen the moon appear, always the same, on the wane, a little lopsided and moving towards the new moon, but this time, when the clouds parted and the moon appeared in the sky, it seemed different, slightly more lopsided, I thought, as if it had shrunk very slightly. And suddenly I had a glimpse of hope: a moon on the wane, moving in the right direction, a time that had begun to pass.

I went on standing there in the cold air as yet another cloud drifted over the moon, but when it had passed the moon that appeared looked exactly as it always did and my hope evaporated. It hadn't changed. I had been mistaken, it was still the moon of the eighteenth of November and I went back to the house, slipped inside, wiped my wet feet on the mat, came into my room and closed the door as quietly as I could.

But it struck me that something had changed. The hope of a return to progressive time has become a surprise that appears in the middle of the night. An ambush, a rare glimpse, there for a moment then gone again.

I could feel the mood coming on. First a feeling of sadness, a touch of gloom falling over my thoughts, shadows of a sort, but flickering in a way that could tip over into gentle mirth. Back in bed I was conscious of this tenuous sorrow which, only a moment later, caused me to give a soft, hesitant laugh, as if I didn't know whether it was me or the world that was laughable. It was like when you are made a fool of or are the butt of a joke. Suddenly you see yourself from the outside and you can't help joining in the laughter anyway.

Recalling the way I felt last night, that sense of change and hope, and then my dismay at the rude reversion to the same lopsided moon, I cannot help but feel that the world's been pulling my leg. That not only was I mistaken, but that I had fallen for an April Fool's prank. As if the moon had altered its appearance just long enough for me to imagine that there really was a difference, only then to act all innocent, just hanging there in the sky, totally deadpan. It makes me chuckle very quietly to see how easily tricked I could be: a dupe, falling for the firmament's April Fool hoax. Thanks, moon.

146

I have fallen into a rhythm. I wake up in the morning. I hear Thomas in the house. I stay still when the house is quiet. I move about when his sounds will blot me out. I boil water in my kettle when he has gone upstairs, when he turns on the bathroom tap, when he flushes the toilet. The water filling the cistern blankets my sounds. The printer churning out letters and labels blocks out the noise of boiling kettles. I go about the house when Thomas is out. We have a rhythm, we complement one another. It is a rhythm that must not be broken. I go out under cover of the music, when the doors I open are lost in sound. I open rustly carrier bags when rustly carrier bags cannot be heard.

I have not found a way out of the eighteenth of November, but I have found roads and paths through the day, narrow passages and tunnels I can move along. I cannot get out, but I can find ways in.

I find my way into a predictable world, a pattern that acquires more and more details. I flow in and out of the house. I flow through the day. I am fluid. I let myself flow with the sounds, like a liquid, and liquids flow in to fill any available space.

I hear Thomas's footsteps around the house. There is hardly

any distance between us. I count days, but they no longer make the distance greater. I have found my way into his day. We move as one, in harmony, we are playing a duet, or we are an entire orchestra. We have the rain and the shifting light. We have the sound of cars driving past, of the birds in the garden, we have the water gushing through the pipes in the house.

It is easier now. If I follow his day, if I maintain the rhythm, if I don't disrupt the pattern. If I wake at the sound of footsteps on the stairs. If I boil water when he is printing out labels for our letters and parcels. I have the sounds and his movements. It is merely time that is broken. We are together. With only some walls in a house separating us. There are no dead, no injured, and that is not something we talk about. Words are not necessary. There are syllables and there is rhythm. I hear the rhythm in the house, footsteps on the stairs. I hear stressed and unstressed raindrops on the windowpane. Music is necessary. For rhythm and rain-wet syllables. It is something that can be heard: we are a quiet orchestra and we are playing now. Listen.

151

When Thomas is in the kitchen I can hear the connections between us. He sends messages and plays music all through the house. He sends messages I understand. They sound like running water, like metal on metal, like fridge doors bumping against worktops, but these are concerts he is playing and I play too, very softly.

The distance is greatest when he is in the living room and I sometimes have the urge to transcend the distance, I feel like getting up and opening the door and ruining everything, disrupting our rhythm. But I know that if I went in there the distance between us would grow even greater and so I don't go in there. I do not go in and toss 151 days onto the floor in a heap between us. I do not go into that room and try to drag him out of his pattern. I live with the distance. I sit on the bed and read. I know that he will soon come closer again. Why would I toss 151 days onto the floor in a heap when I can have this very short distance?

When Thomas is in the hall he is too close, but that passes. He carries teacups from place to place. He takes coats off pegs and picks up parcels from floors. I breathe easy. I am safe. He won't come in here. He won't come in and find his 151 forgotten days. He draws near, but he passes the door. I am safe. From the days that pile up between us. From Thomas and all his forgetting.

I can hear footsteps on the stairs and in a moment I will hear him moving around upstairs. He doesn't feel far away, because each step is transmitted through the ceiling like a whisper through the fabric of the house. Only when he is in the living room is he too far away and only in the hall is he too close.

The distance is shortest at night. When Thomas is asleep there is only the ceiling between us, a thin line between two forms of time. I sit in a room that holds the world open and keeps the distance between us as short as possible. He calls the ceiling the floor. I call the floor the ceiling. But these are just words, not a distance but a line that keeps us connected.

It is just a house with rooms. There is someone in the house. His name is Thomas Selter and he moves from room to room. He plays music with his patterns. Who is he playing for? He is playing for me.

157

It is easy to get the days to pass. They fly by. I want, but it is a light wanting. I yearn, but it is an easy yearning. It is a day containing more and more details. It is becoming more and more predictable. I feel at home. I feel at home in more and more details. I know how the day goes. I know its sounds and the intervals between the sounds. I know the shifts in the light and the intensity of the rain. I see the light opening up the room when the sun breaks through. There is a blackbird's zig-zagging flight call and the muffled drone of a car two streets away and later the same sounds in a different order: light, car, bird. Later again: wind in trees, plant pot in wind, brief pause, car. And later still: wind, plant pot, long pause, car. And before I know it the day is over.

164

It is easy to get the days to pass if I relax. Or rather: I don't get the days to do anything. They do it all by themselves. I don't need to do anything except write a number in the notebook in the morning. I don't need to say anything about the days, the paper lies there, blank, and time passes more quickly if I don't say anything. I flow through the days, something or someone flows. I breathe. I tell myself that sentences are no longer necessary. I hear the day follow its patterns and before I know it the day is over.

176

The pace seems to have sped up, not much, there is no sudden acceleration or headlong rush, it is quite gradual and I do nothing but follow the day and before I know it the day is over.

179

The days flow and I flow with them. I wake up and follow my pattern and before I know it the day is over.

180

I count the days. One by one they vanish as soon as they have arrived. I write the number of the day in my notebook and before I know it, it is over. I don't know why the days have to be counted, but I don't dare not to. I tell myself that I have to hold on to the days. Maybe there is help to be had from the columns of numbers. Like a rope you could use to haul yourself out of a well if you fall in. But if there's no one there to hold on to the other end of the rope there is no help to be had. You're never going to get out anyway.

181

It is dark and still down here. Maybe it is the feeling of light-headedness that helps the days to pass. From the lack of oxygen. The air is damp and although it may be hard to believe the day contains so many details that the time flies by. You would think the dark wouldn't have details, but that is only if you don't count the sounds. Or the light glimpsed up there. A little snippet of sky. Perhaps I'm simply waiting for the rope to become long enough, for it to accumulate enough days to be heavy enough to throw, for it to land up there, for it to reach all the way down here, for someone to spot it and start to pull me up. How many days would it take?

185

And yet sometimes I find myself thinking that maybe this will be the day. Maybe I will wake to the nineteenth. Or maybe it won't be the nineteenth. Maybe there are weeks and months lying under my eighteenth of November. Maybe, if I relax and let the days flow. Maybe the days will rise to the surface like bubbles and all at once it will be May or June and I will wake to morning light and be blown away by the singing of the birds. Or I will wake up in August, to a late summer morning and everything will sound different. I will wake to Thomas on the stairs. To stairs that creak the way old stairs creak when it has been summer for long enough.

Suddenly I remember the sounds of summer. I remember the creaking of the stairs. You don't hear it when there is moisture in the air, it is never there in the winter, but there comes a point in the course of the summer when the stairs start to creak. It has to do with the wood drying out and you have to tread carefully, especially if you're going up or down the stairs when someone is sleeping. If it is the middle of the night or early in the morning, when all else is still and when the dry creak fills the room if you don't set your feet very carefully and silently on step after step after step. It is a sound that speaks of summer and the many years those stairs have been there, of the generations of feet they have carried up and down. But when summer is over, in the middle of September or some time in October, the sound disappears from the stairs, the moisture seeps back into the wood and autumn sets in with its breezes and silent stairs.

Now I am thinking about the sounds of the year. About sounds that are gone and of sounds that are sleeping. I want the year to wake up. To come back, to bubble up into my eighteenth of November. But all I can do is relax and let the days flow. Give time the peace in which to resume its normal course. It helps not to make any noise. That is not how you rouse a year. All I can do is leave the day to gradually awaken, somewhere underneath the eighteenth of November. Sentences are not necessary, nor are columns of numbers. What is necessary is peace and quiet. Ssh.

186

But if sentences are not necessary why do I sit down at the table and write about the summer creaking? And if counting the days does not help why do I write a new number every morning when I hear Thomas putting the kettle on the stove?

Maybe my sentences are no more than repeated calls to an emergency service where no one answers the phone. Little attempts to leave a message for someone who never calls back.

Maybe my columns of numbers are not, in fact, a rope that I can use to climb out of a well, maybe I am already out and the column of numbers is a rail for me to hold on to as I walk along the edge of a precipice. If I miss a day there will be a gap in my rail and I will fall over the edge. So I write down a number every morning and walk along my precipice. But where are we going? And when will someone answer?

199

I was afraid this would happen and now it has. Several times. I have started following Thomas. I get ready to go out when I hear the music in the living room. I walk down to the supermarket, I do my shopping as usual, but then I find myself heading for the post office. I see him go in and I wait outside till he emerges then I follow him almost all the way down to the woods before turning around, hurrying back to the house and making up my mind not to write about it and not to do it again.

204

It doesn't happen every day. I try not to, but sometimes I can't resist it. I go out to do my shopping, along my own paths, paths which Thomas doesn't take. But then I turn down into the town. I make my way to the market and suddenly I remember our strolls through town together, doing our shopping at familiar stalls, chatting to stallholders who have traded in the square for years and known Thomas since he was a boy, and the stallholders say hello and ask after Thomas. Then I remember how we would call in at La Petite Èchelle, I must go and get him, I tell myself, take him there, so we can sit in the café while it rains, then I think of him walking around freely only a few streets away. I take roads I ought to avoid, I turn wrong corners, I follow his usual routes, I catch sight of him farther along the street, I see him disappear through the yellow post-office door, I wait, I draw back slightly into one of the narrow side streets across from the post office, I can see him through the post-office windows, I see him come out. I start to follow him then do an abrupt about-turn. And decide, yet again, not to.

207

But it happens anyway. I follow him at a distance, he walks along the road, carrying letters and parcels, I stay well back, but still I feel I am too close. Nonetheless, I narrow the gap slightly, see him open the door and go inside.

I feel my legs buckling, my feet tingling, my hands tingling. I go hot and cold, feel breathless and almost dizzy, I mean to turn around, but instead I cross the street and walk along the pavement on the opposite side from the post office. I can see him in there. I do my best to breathe slowly and deeply.

108

If I crane my neck I can see everything through the window. He is talking to someone behind the counter, a woman. She seems quite unfazed, as if she doesn't know how lucky she is. To be able to speak to him as if nothing has happened. So casually. To be so close. To be able to see his face. To be able to look up. And not faint clean away.

I hurry past, so I won't be seen. I mean to keep on walking, but instead I find myself crossing the street. I approach the door. The panes in the door are set in yellow steel frames, the glass is frosted and he is only a shadow beyond the door, but I know where he is standing. I can see a silhouette and Thomas is that silhouette.

I take a few steps to the side, attempt to walk on, then turn and go back to the door. I reach out my hand and grasp the handle. The door is heavy, I feel it resist, but then it opens. He has placed his parcels on the counter. I hear the woman's voice, a few soft words, a question, I think, and a second later Thomas replying. But I can't stand there any longer. At the sound of his voice I back away and let go of the door handle. I stagger, put a hand to the wall to steady myself, then turn and walk past the windows without looking through them.

I don't see him come out and I'm sure that he doesn't see me either because I am already heading off down the street in the opposite direction. But I hear the door closing behind him. The door closing after a parcel-less Thomas. Thomas leaving the post office. Thomas letting go of a yellow steel door. To be a door. To be touched. And slowly swing back into place and close on easy hinges.

But that's not me. I don't swing shut. I have no hinges. There is nothing to hold on to. I stop short and turn slightly as he vanishes around the corner and then I stand there like that, kind of twisted around, because I can't move my legs, but I can turn my body and see him vanish around the corner.

He doesn't see me. He doesn't see me there, twisted around and he doesn't see me straightening up or, moments later, slowly walking off, because he is going the other way, around the corner and towards the woods, and I don't follow him because I have enough to do just staying upright, I take a few steps, then stop and put my hand to the wall.

It is the loss that staggers me. It is the longing for what is lost and there is nothing I can do about it.

Only if I confine myself to the sounds can I cope with the loss. Then I can think clearly, then I can try to find a solution, an answer, a way out. I can sit in this room and get the days to pass one after another.

219

I don't follow Thomas any more. It did happen on a couple of other occasions, but I don't do it any more. I have been out in the garden once in the evening. I have seen him through the living-room window. On the windowsill is a bust that Thomas inherited from his grandfather, of whom I don't know, but it sits in such a way that a person can hide behind it. I have stood behind it, ready to retreat if Thomas should turn and look out of the window, but he doesn't turn and now I know how he moves about the living room. I have seen him sitting down in the armchair with his book. I know when he will get up again and when he will go through to the kitchen. I have stood in the darkness and seen him get up from his chair and put wood on the fire before leaving the living room. I have seen the smoke rising from the chimney in the rain. You can see it if you step back a bit and look up, but that can only be done when Thomas is in the kitchen. Then you can take a few paces back, two paces, three paces, maybe four, and there it is, a thin trail of smoke coiling up from the chimney, visible in the glow of the street lamp on the other side of the house, and if I move even further back I can see the whole house, with lights in the windows, I can see a light in the guest room, but no one is in there.

While I was in the garden it started to rain so I retreated to the tool shed and sat there, waiting for Thomas to go upstairs. I sat on a wooden crate with the door open to the garden and when the light falling on the garden changed slightly I knew that he had switched on the lamp up there. I left the shed, gently opened the back door and slipped inside, and as soon as I heard him flush the toilet upstairs I closed the door and locked it with a faint click, opened the spare-room door, stepped inside and closed it behind me.

But I no longer do that. I don't follow him and I don't watch him through the night-time windows. The distance grows when I can see him. I flow more easily through the day when I follow my rhythm. His rhythm. Our rhythm. When I listen to his movements, when I follow the music and let myself be led through the day. I wake in the morning, I listen and follow the sounds and before I know it the day is over.

223

I have discovered something uncanny. Or at least, it's not something I have discovered, because I already knew it, but I have discovered that it is uncanny. It's a problem I cannot solve. There are ghosts and monsters. Thomas is the ghost and I am the monster.

Each evening, when Thomas has returned home in the rain, when he has hung up his coat in the hall, when he has changed into dry clothes and hung the wet ones over a radiator upstairs, when he has put wood on the fire in the living room and relit it, when he has done all of this, as his pattern dictates, he comes to the next point. He pulls on a pair of wellingtons because his shoes are by the fireside, still wet, but the wellingtons are just inside the front door, so he puts them on, opens the door, cuts across the front garden and around to the garden shed. He rummages around a bit in there. I think he's looking for a spade but he can't find it, so instead he takes a trowel that is hanging by its leather loop from a hook on the wall. Armed with this he goes back out into the garden. It is raining very softly as he hurries along the garden path, down to the bed of leeks and Swiss chard, sticks the trowel deep into the ground next to a nice fat leek, works it free and pulls it out, bangs the trowel against a stone to knock off some soil, hurries back to the shed, hangs up the trowel, grabs some onions from a box and a shallot from a string bag hanging from the ceiling, comes out of the shed, past the kitchen window and through the door, shuts the door and carries the leek and onions into the kitchen.

This is pure routine. These are the things that make up his day. He digs up a leek in a garden. He fetches onions from a shed. I know, because I have seen the hole in the earth left by the leek and the vestiges of fresh soil on the trowel hanging in the shed. I have heard him in the garden and I have heard the clink of metal on stone, because I was standing on the other side of the house listening while he was out there and I have seen a flat rock spattered with small clods of earth, the dirt dissolving in the rain.

Back in the house he takes two carrots from the bottom of the fridge, he finds a stock cube, he chops onions – I know, because I have seen onion peelings and carrot shavings in the compost bin. He is making soup and for that he needs his leek. He slices it finely, diagonally – I know, because he always slices vegetables diagonally – then he rinses his sliced leeks in a bowl of water and adds them to his soup to simmer.

There is nothing odd about that, apart from the fact that every morning, when it grows light, the leek is back where it was. In the row at the bottom of the garden, untouched, unpicked, unsliced, ready to be lifted out of the ground. That's the way things are and I have got used to that thought.

Yesterday afternoon, while Thomas was out, I picked a leek from the other end of the row. Then I boiled water, dissolved a bit of stock cube in it and added the finely sliced leek. I cooked my thin soup and ate it by the window in the living room.

Today that leek is gone. As leeks usually are, of course, when dug up, sliced, cooked and eaten. I have been out in the garden, I went down to the vegetable plot and that leek isn't there in the row. This shouldn't have surprised me, but suddenly it seemed all wrong. That was how things were when we were together. Once things had been eaten they were gone. We took things from the world. But when Thomas is on his own nothing disappears. It was me who made things disappear. That must be it. I am living in a time that eats up the world.

Without me Thomas's day returns, the world is repaired, the leek is back in the row, and I'm sure it's the same with the onions. There were too many in the shed for me to tell, but if I were to go and check I'm sure it would be the same story with them. I could count them, if I really wanted to know, but I don't need to. I already know. I know that if I take onions from the shed for myself they will disappear. I know because I have seen who we are: Thomas is a ghost and I am a monster. That's the way things are. It is time that has done this. Without me Thomas is a ghost, but I am a monster, a beast, a pest.

It's not that I didn't know this. It's not that I haven't seen the shelves growing barer and barer, but now it's a problem. It makes a difference. If Thomas is a ghost and I am a monster then the distance between us is greater than I thought. Thomas leaves no trail in the world, I eat it up. He is a pattern in the house, I am a monster in the guest room. If I go out there we will be two monsters. I will drag him into my world and we will eat for two. It is me who makes the difference. He is a ghost and ghosts haunt. They return, again and again. Monsters rampage through the world and leave it devastated. I sit in this room overlooking the garden and a woodpile. I don't do much. But still I am using up the world while Thomas lives in a world that restores itself. I leave a trail. I have become a ravening monster, a monster in a finite world. A swarm of locusts. How long can my little world endure me?

224

I can no longer flow through the day. It seems to have grown too small, either that or I have grown too heavy. To have grown huge and shapeless. A monster cannot flow in and out of a day, a monster is not fluid. It cannot flow into and fill the day's empty spaces. It overflows. It grows. It cannot hide in the world. A monster rumbles. It rampages. It cannot be still. It cannot play in a quiet orchestra. A monster is slow and heavy. The days begin to go more slowly. I fill. I do not flow. It is me who is slowing things down.

225

But then, maybe we are both ghosts, I think. Hopefully. Maybe it's all a hallucination. I am a ghost that thinks it is a monster. Thomas is a ghost that thinks it is a person. We are two of a kind. I think again. Hopefully. We live in a world of ghosts. With ghostly leeks that disappear or return. We are two of a kind. Not monsters or people, just ghosts that think they are monsters or people. Who fill space for no one or fill space for two.

Or I am asleep in a bed in a hotel in Paris, dreaming that I am a monster, devouring my world in a time that stands still. When will I wake up? Wake me.

226

But it is no use. I cannot tell myself that this is only a dream. Whenever I do that I fill my world with other scenarios. I imagine that we're both dead and that the whole thing is the fantasy of hovering souls, or I imagine that Thomas left the eighteenth of November long ago and has travelled on without me. To the nineteenth and the twentieth, to December and January and February and March. I imagine that I am roaming through a world of shadows while everyone else has carried on as if time were intact.

But why would he have travelled on? He is still here. I can hear him on the stairs. He is here, but we are no longer an orchestra. We are not two of a kind because I am a monster, consuming my world.

I can feel the slowness of the day now. I am not a liquid that flows through the day, filling the empty spaces and flowing on into the next day. We are not an orchestra, playing our way through the day. We are not two people in a dance through a house, we are not two ghosts dreaming different dreams and we are not music, we are a monster and a ghost, I can feel the walls tightening around me as I swell and I am no longer sure if there is space for me here.

227

It is the words that do it. We started out as two lovers in a misty landscape. Giddy travellers. We did our shopping and drank coffee at some point in the eighteenth of November. We fried eggs in the kitchen and picked orange-flavoured chocolate off a shelf in the supermarket and things disappeared and I am a pest, a monster that devours my world. I pick vegetables in the garden and the garden disappears. I chew and chew. There is munching and crunching and foaming at the mouth. Drool running from the corners of my mouth. Down my chin. The rubbish piles up. Shelves grow barer and barer. The monster lurches on, day after day. Munching, crunching. When I chew my crispbread I hear the noise of it in my head. You sound like a horse, I tell myself, like a horse crunching carrots. A cat chewing its dry food. A dog gnawing a bone, a rabbit at its food bowl, a swarm of insects munching its way through forests and fields. I am all of these, I am hordes of chomping creatures. Munching, crunching, chewing. A zoo, an overcrowded barn, a buzzing swarm.

I hear Thomas going up the stairs. He leaves no trail. He buys and buys and still nothing happens. He slices bread and chops leeks. He rustles along with his carrier bags, he moves around the house and sets his feet on every single step on the stairs, but it is as if he has never been there. I hear him in the bath-room. A ghost peeing upright. Pure pissing spirit. What sort of a world is this?

It is the words that make the difference. I thought 'monster' and now I am growing. Who am I now? Am I a monster or simply a person in a room? Am I a pest or just a two-legged, sentient being with far too much time in her day? What do I hear? Do I hear my darling passing water, do I hear my husband peeing, do I hear the sound of a urinating ghost, do I hear anything at all? Not much. All is quiet here. He has flushed the toilet, the cistern has filled, water has gushed through the pipes, the picture is complete. He is taking a break or he has evaporated, like pure consciousness, living air. But I hope I will hear him again in a minute or two, when he comes down the stairs.

It is my mood that chooses the words for me. I have a mood. There is a lot you can do with such a thing. It can select words from the whole lexical palette, it can call language a palette, it can give things colours, even when they have no colours. I talk to no one, but my world acquires more and more details, I pluck words from a world with many voices, from a mood that lends colour, that rubs off. But lending colour to things takes up space. The palette overflows with hues. Too many words pour in, the day becomes heavier, slower, comes to a halt.

Ah, now the peeing ghost is coming down its stairs.

228

I do my shopping farther away now. I can't go on using the supermarket in the rue Clémentine Giroux. I have already seen the results of that: bare shelves and empty spaces in cool cabinets. There's nothing new in that. It was noted during our foggy days, it is well documented, it was tested and recorded during the days of our observations. But now I see signs of it everywhere I have been. More things are disappearing. All the caramel-flavoured chocolate has been eaten up. Some of the bread baskets are now empty and on the bottom shelf in the bread section there are only two packs of biscotti surrounded by thin air because I have taken the rest. Several sorts of cheese have vanished from the cheese section, there are no tomatoes in the fresh produce aisle and there is no ignoring the great dents that have been made in the shelves. I did this, it has happened gradually, one day at a time.

I try to spread my shopping. I seek out shops I haven't used before. I change my habits and eat things I don't normally eat. I choose my purchases according to what there is the most of and which shelves are the fullest and buy unknown tins of fish, bags of weird powdered soups or biscuits I've never tasted.

I think of the future. I have begun to look at gardens, at plots which still have vegetables in them, at apple trees with fruit on the branches, at grapes that haven't yet been picked, even though it is November. I steal glances at the ground under the walnut trees in the gardens. I am looking for pieces of the world that nobody will use. Surplus. I have begun to picture a future for myself as a wanderer, roaming from place to place, a vagabond, picking up a little bit here and there, buying a little bit here and there and travelling on, leaving next to no trail. I envisage this going on for a long time. That there could be many eighteenths of November to come. I know that if I take to foraging in gardens I will be stealing from the birds, the worms. But, I tell myself, if I can't make the fault in time disappear, if things are never going to be any different ... but then I realise that I've thought too far, so I don't think any farther.

229

Occasionally I consider finding somewhere else to live.
I think about Thomas's grandfather who never moved
from the house where he had lived with Thomas's grand-
mother. Who lived here alone for seventeen years before
he himself died. Who always lived the same life, followed
the same rhythm. Who grew the same vegetables, in the
same amounts, according to a scheme that still hangs in the
shed and that we have endeavoured to follow. To switch
from carrots and parsley to sweetcorn and courgettes, from
sweetcorn and courgettes to beans and peas and, the next
year, to leeks and Swiss chard and possibly cabbage the year
after that. He explained it all to Thomas every year and,
later, to me too, when we visited him. How the year was
shaping up this time around and what that meant for next
year's rotation. How the soil fared with different crops.
How different plants fared together, about the partnerships
between plants, about how helpful marigolds could be and
how dill and fennel preferred to have their own space. And
Thomas would listen patiently, even though he'd heard it
all many times before. But after his wife died old Selter had
to keep neighbours and friends supplied with vegetables
because the garden produced too much for one person.

How do they live in the same houses, though, those couples
who have been halved? How do they go on living the same
life year after year? In the same rooms, with the same day-
to-day routine. How do they do it? Do they go on doing the

same things, because the house is the same? Do they retreat into a single room? Do they sit there and suddenly have the idea that they can hear the dead walking about? Are the dead too close or too far away? Do they hear steps in the distance or a hand or sleeve brushing the wallpaper? Do they think there are ghosts in the house? Do they think they are monsters when the other half has stopped eating? That it is a mistake that they are still in the world? Do they think that they should work the soil, that they should continue to get the garden to yield roots and fruits and greens?

But I cannot work the soil. I have one single rainy day. I harvest nothing. I sow nothing. Nothing is sprouting or growing. My seasons are gone. Nothing comes of my days. They merely pass and I follow them and eat up my world and listen to the ghost in the house.

230

I don't know if there's space for a monster in this room. The day has slowed down, my world has shrunk or I have grown, I don't know which. I don't go through the day as lightly as I used to, my movements are noisy. The sounds I make in here are not music, I am not a member of a quiet orchestra. The sounds Thomas makes and the music from the living room fill the house, but I am not playing in the orchestra.

I do not follow Thomas. He goes for his walks through the woods and down by the river. He returns home in the rain while I am in my room and sometimes I look up and see a shadow opening a gate and closing it behind it.

232

Last night I had the sudden urge to go outside. Not because I wanted to watch Thomas through the window. It was the middle of the night and he had long since gone to bed. I needed the loo because I had drunk more tea than usual and had woken out of a dream in which I was looking for a toilet, but every time I found one it was occupied. The door was always slightly ajar so I would think it was vacant, but every time I pushed the door open there was someone sitting on the loo.

When I woke from my dream I went over to the window. I wanted to see if it was raining. But no, the clouds had passed, leaving a broad belt of clear sky in which the moon was visible, the same moon as always, on the wane. It never changes and I no longer imagine that I can see any change. The sky is the same, it changes in the course of the night, as skies do, but the following night everything is the same again.

All of a sudden I felt like sitting out there. I grabbed a blanket and my duvet, then I went around to the shed and got a cushion from a garden chair and placed this on the back-door step along with the duvet and the blanket. After peeing behind the gooseberry bushes in the vegetable plot I arranged myself on the step with my back against the door and the blanket and duvet wrapped around me. Another swathe of cloud had drifted across the moon, but once this had passed the moon shone down brightly on my duvet there in the darkness.

The wind had died down. The plastic plant pot I had heard rolling about night after night was still there on the cobbles at the side of the house, but it was hardly moving at all. I can't have been out at that time before, because there was less noise and more sky to be seen than on other occasions when I had been out at night. For nearly an hour I watched the clouds drifting by with one large clear stretch of sky after another revealed in between.

Occasionally I would hear the sound of a car, sometimes nearby, but more often only as a faint drone in the distance. Otherwise there were few sounds, apart from the soft rustling of the trees and the discreet clitter-clatter of the plant pot, which I suddenly found intrusive, with its muted agitation, its plastic tattoo on the cobbles.

Nevertheless, I fell asleep, sitting with my back to the closed door and my duvet wrapped around me. I must have shifted in my sleep, however, because suddenly I woke up, having bumped my head against the stone door frame. It was still dark, but I quickly picked up my things and tiptoed back to my bed. And now here I am, waking to a day that has long since begun.

233

The first thing that struck me when I sat down outside in the dark was the silence. Once again I had woken up in the middle of the night and had the urge to see the night sky. But this time I felt there was something different about the garden. It took me a while to figure out what it was, but then it dawned on me that the sound of the plant pot rolling about in the wind was missing.

And then I remembered that I had picked up the pot on my way to the shed to put back the cushion from the garden chair after my nocturnal visit. I seemed to recall putting the pot on a shelf in the shed, but I had been half-asleep and wasn't entirely certain so I got up to check and sure enough, there it was, sitting, or lying almost, on the top of a box containing twine and gardening gloves and packets of seeds.

I went back to the step, where I had again arranged myself with cushion and duvet, as well as an old rug underneath me to ward off the dampness. It surprised me that the plant pot had not simply reverted to its activity of the eighteenth, careening back and forth on the cobbles. It had nothing to do with me, it had been clattering about there all on its own, so why should it stop? I'm sure I've picked up that pot once before and put it away in the shed, when I was with Thomas, during the days of our investigations, and I'm sure that it was back on its spot the next day. But now it had consented to being moved, it had allowed me to stop it from rolling around on the cobbles and it was quite clear that a sound was now missing.

I very quickly gave up trying to come up with an explanation for this and returned to the predictable patterns of the night sky. There is something reassuring about the sky. It is not like books or plant pots. It is not like tins of olives or packets of biscuits. There is nothing to be done about it. It can be relied upon. It never changes. I cannot influence it and I cannot spoil it. It brooks no intrusion by me, it does not care about monsters on steps. It is full of movement, of objects passing by, but nothing that clatters and even if there were sounds up there, if there were such things as harmonies of the spheres or celestial melodies, they would never be heard down here. The distance is far too great.

I gazed at the stars and the droves of clouds whose patterns I felt I already knew. A single cloud flitted across the moon just as a larger cluster of clouds hove into view above the trees on the other side of the road. A cloud couple, a single cloud, another single cloud, a double couple, two clusters moving as one. I felt I had seen this before, and at that same moment a cloud passed close to the moon, which was hanging directly above a mobile phone mast in the distance. The cloud slipped by without touching the top of the moon and sitting there at my lookout post I was sure that these cloud movements were exactly the same as the night before, only without the plant pot.

The sky has its pattern. It repeats itself. You can feel at home with it. You can sit on a step in the darkness and observe it or you can stand on the grass and be a very tiny monster in an immense space. I can feel the sky lifting the monster cape from my shoulders. I become smaller and the little pieces of the world that I have to work with dwindle to almost nothing. The heavens are vast and untouchable, the universe opens up and you become an insignificant little monster taking tiny bites out of a gigantic world.

I sat there for a long time. Wakeful and warm on my step. I beheld droves of clouds, small groups and lonesome wanderers. Sharp silhouettes or soft, amorphous masses with fraying edges, travelling singly or in pairs through the night, past stars whose names I didn't know.

It is good that the sky has opened up. It is good that the world has regained its sense of proportion. That it cannot be disturbed by little pests scurrying about in the darkness. It is good to know of a place where nothing can be accomplished.

I need to study the sky. I want to get to know it. I want names and patterns. It is good to know that I can come back night after night. That I can get to know the heavens. That I cannot damage the mechanism. It is good that the world stands still.

234

How can I say it is good that the world stands still? How can I say it is good that it doesn't move, that there is nothing I can accomplish, that nothing happens? How can that be good? How can it be good that Thomas is slowly being carried farther and farther away? That we are not travelling together? How can I say that? Maybe I should think twice before I write. Anything. Here.

245

Today I bought a telescope. I left the house when Thomas was out for the first time. There is nowhere in Clairon to buy a telescope, of course. Nevertheless, I went to the electronics superstore out on the ring road, but there I was told there was no great demand for telescopes. I could buy flat-screen TVs, I could buy loudspeakers and white goods. I could buy laptops and mobile phones and a digital single-lens reflex camera. I could buy a blender or a yogurt maker if I so wished. I could buy an electric kettle or a hotplate, but I bought those a while ago in the ironmonger's in town.

It was strange to be walking around out there by the ring road. It is a long time since I've been any farther away from the house than the town centre and the road around the edge of the woods. I left the shop empty-handed and ready to abandon my plan altogether and go home, but Thomas would long since have got back with his carrier bags and it would be hard to get in without being heard.

So instead I turned down towards the station. It was raining slightly, I had put up my umbrella and suddenly I remembered my trek home on my second eighteenth of November. I had the same bag slung over my shoulder, it was lighter now, because there were no books in it. I had left them at the house. And suddenly I felt a twinge of doubt: I was walking away. I had left Thomas and the books in the house. What would there be to come back to, I wondered briefly, but when I got to the station there were only four minutes till the next train to Lille. I grabbed a ticket from the machine, dashed onto the platform and jumped on the train before I could change my mind.

The train was half empty. It was mid-morning and there weren't many people taking the Lille train from Clairon. I hadn't given much thought to my appearance. Occasionally, when I'm out, I will glance in a shop window to make sure that I look like a human being, but I had never considered the risk of suddenly finding myself sitting opposite someone on a train. Not a passer-by on the street or a shop assistant reeling off questions and following well-worn routines, but a person with time. A seated person, positioned right in front of me, possibly with their face turned in my direction. All at once I found this a daunting prospect and I regretted getting on the train.

Fortunately, there were only two other people in the carriage I had chosen and there was plenty of room for all three of us. I sat where I could only see the arm of the one person and the suitcase of the other, no faces. Still, though, I went to the toilet before we reached the first station. I made sure that I looked normal, that I looked like a human being of sorts and not a monster, a creature out on shady business, a visitor from other galaxies or a person inhabiting a totally different time, but not many other passengers boarded the train so I needn't have worried.

In Lille I was struck by a strange feeling of euphoria. Shortly after arriving there I found a shop selling ornithological equipment, with birdwatching binoculars and books and so on, but also cameras and telescopes of all types. Unhindered by any financial considerations as I was, I was tempted to buy both an advanced telescope and a quiet camera with a telephoto lens, but I managed to curb my euphoric impulse and ended up buying a good serviceable telescope which I had spotted in the shop window even before I hesitantly allowed myself to be ushered inside by a customer who held the door open for me.

Ideal for beginners, but still a first-class instrument, the assistant said when I expressed my wish to buy a relatively uncomplicated telescope. It was durable, he said, and a good buy. I must have looked like a sensible sort of individual, but that wasn't how I felt. I had the urge to buy more of their instruments and might have taken up photography or birdwatching or examining the objects of the world through a sophisticated microscope had it not been for the fact that it would have seemed too noteworthy. I obviously belonged to a very different segment: prudent and level-headed, not impetuous or eager to study the world's phenomena with the greatest possible precision.

As a bonus for making my sensible purchase he offered me an astronomical atlas containing a brief introduction to those stars and planets visible through an ordinary telescope like the one I had bought. I didn't say that I already had a copy of *The Heavenly Bodies* from 1767. I don't think he would have considered it contemporary enough.

I paid and prepared to leave the shop with my telescope: duly unpacked, demonstrated, taken apart then folded up and laid in an odd trumpet-shaped case, along with a tripod and various other attachments: not very discreet, but easy to carry. Halfway out the door I stopped, let go of the door handle, turned and asked if I could leave the telescope over in a corner of the shop while I ran a few errands. The assistant said that would be all right, so I left it there and walked back out onto the street.

I spent the next couple of hours picking up groceries with a haste I did not recognise from my days in the house. I visited seven or eight shops, I bought several different varieties of coffee and tea, I bought confit de canard, tins of fish, packs of cheese with expiry dates far into the future and a few well-aged artisan cheeses which, according to the cheesemonger, would keep well outside of the fridge. In a health-food shop I bought a selection of vegetable pâtés in cans and jars. I bought almonds, other nuts and seeds. I bought cartons and cans of beans, peas and sweetcorn, and with every purchase I felt relief at the very small dent I was making in global food stocks: my raids left hardly any visible effect on the shops.

At a stationer's I bought a notebook, hardback with an olive-green cloth binding. Lined paper and stitched spine. It hasn't been put to use yet, but I feel I am moving towards something new which has not quite started.

When I was finished I withdrew as much cash as I possibly could on my credit card, hailed a taxi, piled all of my shopping into the car and asked the driver to take me to the shop where I had left my telescope. I collected it, loaded it into the boot of the taxi and asked the driver to take me to Clairon: a little over an hour's drive in weather that alternated between sunshine, grey skies and the odd shower. We reached the house well before Thomas was due to return, while it was still dry out and before it began to get dark.

Back at the house I paid the taxi fare and proceeded to carry my bags first into the hall and then into my room. The house was cold, the embers in the grate having died out as usual and no one had switched on the heating. I turned up the thermostat, a little higher than I normally did because I suddenly felt cold.

Under the bed I found two plastic storage boxes containing spare bed linen, which I took out and laid on the bottom shelf of the bookcase next to the bed. I put as much of my shopping as I could into the plastic boxes and the rest into a cardboard box which I had found in the garden shed, then I pushed the whole lot back under the bed.

It began to get dark while I was folding up the last empty carrier bags and when the rain became heavier I retreated to my room. From the window I could see our neighbour hurrying past the fence at the bottom of the garden. Shortly afterwards I heard Thomas arrive home and a moment later the light from the hall filtered under my door.

I have had an eventful day and I am tired, but it's a strange energised tiredness. My brain is spinning. I seem to have changed speed and direction, but also and more particularly, size. I have regained my proper proportions. I am not sure if this is because I spend my nights looking at the sky or because I have gone further afield, travelled by train, walked along unfamiliar streets. Perhaps it is simply because I have spread out my purchases and taken only tiny bites out of a gigantic world. I do not take much from this world, I think to myself, not when you consider its size, and I feel as though I have become lighter, more nimble. I can change direction. That's how little the monster is. That's how little difference I make to the world. That's how little the activities of one person matter on the eighteenth of November.

246

My purchases came through. When I woke up this morning they were still there: the boxes under the bed are full, packs of tea and coffee are piled up on the table behind my electric kettle, my stores have been replenished. I feel calm and carefree. The world is still there, I think to myself, and there is hardly any sign that a little pest has been out there raiding.

The only thing that is gone is my green notebook. I had left it on the table, ready for sentences, observations and reflections. For healing sentences, disjointed sentences, for doubt and uncertainty, questions and concerns, for hope and moods, colours, whatever. It was supposed to mark a new chapter. A very small monster's life in the universe. Now I don't know whether something new has begun or whether something new will begin, but I do know I need to take a closer look at the sky.

251

These last few nights I have been out with my telescope, late at night, when there is the greatest extent of sky to observe. The air is chilly and damp, but there are enough clear spells for most of the sky to become visible at some point in the course of an hour or two.

I unearthed a woollen dress from the bottom drawer of the chest of drawers in the bedroom, because it is cold out there. I got out scarves and a pair of woollen leggings. I go to bed early in the evening, sleep for a few hours and wake again later in the night. I wait until I am sure that all is quiet in the room above me, then I get ready to go out. Silently or almost silently. With my telescope, with a woollen dress and sweaters and a single blanket to keep me warm while I study the sky of the eighteenth of November.

256

I have discovered new ways through the day. I sleep late and don't get up until Thomas has gone out. I sit in the living room or stay in my room. I open cans and bags. I take nuts and caramels from the boxes under my bed. I wish I could invite Thomas to join the party, but there are 256 days to tell him about, and it would take too long.

I go to bed early in the evening, to be ready for the night, but before I do so I prepare for my encounter with the heavens. I open my astronomical atlas and study the stars and planets. On the bookshelves in the living room I found old Selter's planisphere. It can be rotated to follow the turning of the year so you can always find your section of the sky. I knew it was there and the day after my visit to Lille I fetched it from its shelf. I have set it for the middle of November, it took a couple of days for my setting to stay fixed on the planisphere, but now the disc no longer rewinds during the night. Before that it kept turning back to the spring sky. That must have been the last to be viewed. The chart has probably not been used since Thomas and I looked at one of the springtime constellations when visiting Thomas's grandfather. I can't remember why old

Selter had got out his planisphere or what we wanted to see in the sky, but I remember him turning the disc so we could look at the stars and identify them. It felt like something that had happened in another life, almost as if it was an entirely different sky, a sky that changed as the year went on. But the revolving disc is not needed now, all I need is the autumn sky.

259

I'm starting to feel at home when I go out at night. I look up and feel that this is where I live. On a wet lawn on the eighteenth of November. Under moons and stars and planets. I live under an earth-moon with a whitish-grey landscape, huge and dense and pocked with craters and landing sites. I live under Saturn with its very faint ring, like a mist encircling it. Under Jupiter with all its moons. I can see three of them through the telescope: Io, Europa and Ganymede. Callisto is hidden behind Jupiter, so I don't get to see it and the lesser moons are too small for my telescope. But I locate other heavenly bodies, stars of all sizes, I spot small, dense constellations and great solitary lights. I find Castor and Pollux. I move under Orion. I have discovered the shooting stars of the Leonids. I have located the spot in the firmament from which they launch their small bright streaks. They keep recurring, they can be relied upon and I can stand on the grass, I can adjust the telescope and watch them swooshing very quietly across the lens. I live under the Pleiades, high above and very small, and I lean back, adjust the telescope and swivel it as the clouds move across the sky.

I stay out till late, I feel at home, I look to the south, to the north, to the east and the west. I breathe under the starry sky, I spot constellations, I focus. Then I go back into the house and get into bed. I breathe in a house under a starry sky, I sleep and then I wake to the sounds of the house and think to myself that it will soon be sky time again.

262

Every night, once I have seen enough stars and planets, I carefully carry my telescope and my blanket into the house and put them in my room. I close the garden door and lock it with a very faint click. Then I slip into the spare room and close the door.

I have stood on the grass and gazed at the sky, but I always return. To a house where Thomas is asleep and I am quiet because his pattern could be woken, I might disturb it, I move cautiously. It is Thomas who lives here and I am a guest.

During the day I go by the sounds. Thomas has set a pattern in his house. It was already established when I got back from Paris. Maybe even before that, I tell myself. It is his pattern and I have no place in it. Our days together were an intrusion on his pattern, but I no longer intrude. I listen and I adapt. I hear the water in the pipes. The kettle on the stove. I know the sound of the rain and the sounds from the kitchen and the living room. To Thomas this is just a day, lying between two other days, but to me his simple, ordinary day is a pattern. He does things and takes breaks, he is in or out, he is sound or silence. I fall into his framework. He doesn't know it, but I listen and find my way through his day and at night I dress for the stars. I wear wool, I take on a pelt. I dress for the darkness and I stand on the grass and gaze at the sky and once I have been out I go back inside, I close the door and get into a bed that has grown chilly. But that's okay, I get into bed fully clothed and pull the duvet up around me.

I lie in the guest room, because I am a guest. I lie in bed because I am a sleeper. I have gazed at the sky and I have felt at home under the stars. I am getting to know the night sky. Am I a sheep that gazes at the stars or a very small monster clad in wool?

274

The telescope was a mistake. Or rather, it was a mistake if I thought it could make monsters smaller.

I have been outside every night. I feel at home. I dwell in the darkness and I have stood out there in the belief that I would grow smaller by beholding the staggering scale of the heavens, but that is not how it works. Not with a telescope. You get huge, hungry eyes, you intrude, you invade. You meddle in the affairs of the firmament and I can tell that the more familiar I become with the night sky, the more stars that are identified, the more of the moon's surface I see, the bigger I get. I invade space, I fill the world. That is another way of being a monster. In the darkness. In the garden. With ravenous eyes. A monster clad in wool.

I feel it when I go into the house after a night on the grass. The sky no longer makes me feel like a very small monster. I can feel the spare room tightening around me. Like with clothes one is outgrowing. The childhood winter coat that is too small before spring comes. I think of my sister who would inherit my coat, of the threadbare lining, the tightness across the shoulders.

But I went on growing in that coat and the sleeves became too short, the lining began to fray and my sister helped me to make the holes bigger because if it was still in one piece come the spring it would be put away till the autumn and handed down from me to her. She wanted a new coat, not my old one. So we joined forces, we worked away at it, pulled a bit here, picked a bit there and by the spring the coat was too full of holes for it to be handed down. In the autumn we both got new coats. They were blue and mine was bigger. The sleeves were a little too long, but by the winter I had grown into my coat.

Now I am living in a room in a house that is too tight, I have almost outgrown it and sometimes I wander around the town, looking for a new one.

276

There are empty houses in Clairon. Some of them are for rent, others are for sale and some are only empty because their residents are not home on the eighteenth of November.

I don't know what good it can do, but I have started inspecting these houses more closely. Sometimes I roam the streets in the middle of the night, or I walk around with my umbrella in the twilight at dusk to see if there are lights on in them. And then again later in the evening. I sneak out of the house and take a walk around and some of the dark houses are still dark then. I have gone into gardens and checked for keys in sheds, under a lantern on the doorstep or a plant pot by the back door. Sometimes I strike lucky. I have been inside strange houses in the middle of the night, but I have not found a house where I could live.

279

Today I visited the estate agent on the rue Charlemagne. I went out once Thomas had left the house for the first time. First I went to the estate agent on the place Mignolet. I enquired about some of the houses I had observed on my nocturnal wanderings and two of them were for sale, but the location of neither seems quite right. At the estate agent on the rue Charlemagne I found some other houses and asked to be shown around one of them, but the estate agent didn't have time just then. He suggested that we arrange a viewing for the following day, but when I said that wouldn't be possible for me he suggested that I borrow a key to the house, if I would like to look around it on my own. I said I would. I was given the key, went out into the rain and soon located the house, which lay in the rue de l'Ermitage, one of the roads leading down to the woods, the river and the old watermill, not the way Thomas goes on his walk, but a few streets away from the route he takes.

It was a grey roughcast building. It had a bathroom and kitchen, complete with fridge, cooker and electric kettle, a living room on the ground floor and bedrooms upstairs, with tables and beds and everything. It was obvious that no one had been living there for some time. The fridge door had been left open to save it from growing mouldy, the beds were bare, but otherwise it had everything I needed. I looked around the house for about a quarter of an hour. I would only have to bring my own bedding, my bag, my books, my clothes. And the telescope. And I could move in. It would not be difficult.

On the way back I took a detour past a locksmith and had a spare key cut. It would be hard, I told myself, once I had seen how easy it would be to move into the empty house, it would be hard to move away from Thomas even though all I had were his sounds.

After returning the key I went back to the house in the rue de l'Ermitage. My key fitted. I let myself in and sat down in the living room, which smelled a little musty. The heating had been turned off so the radiators didn't work, but there was electricity and I could buy a fan heater. It started to rain while I was sitting there. It sounded different from at our house, maybe something to do with the slope of the roof or the wind direction, I don't know, but the sound is less drumming, gentler perhaps. It was the middle of the day and I recognised the breaks in the rain. There was a view of fields from the kitchen and on the other side of the house there was a drab little courtyard. I didn't see the neighbours and the house sat in such a way that they were unlikely to notice me if I moved in.

281

Yesterday I visited yet another estate agent. She had time to show me around a house I wanted to look at, and she also suggested a couple of other places I could see straight away. At one house the key was under a flowerpot. This house was better than the one in the rue de l'Ermitage. It didn't smell musty, but the neighbours were too close and their living room overlooked the kitchen. They would start to wonder if someone moved in. I wanted no wondering.

At another house the estate agent fetched the key from a hook in a shed which was full of firewood. I could light a fire here, I thought, and tuck myself up in the living room with a book, but before long all the wood would be used up, little by little I would see it disappear, I would see time pass and the monster consume its world. In the end I decided on the grey house in the rue de l'Ermitage. I bought a fan heater and filled a carrier bag with provisions from my boxes under the bed. I packed the telescope into its case, gathered my various piles of papers together and put them into a black cardboard folder that I had found in the office. I picked up clothes while

Thomas was out, took the bed linen that I had laid on the bottom shelf of the bookcase in the guest room, packed my pile of books and a few others from the bookshelves in the living room into my bag and carried the whole lot to my new house. Then I went back to my room.

I was in a quandary. Sitting in the guest room I felt doubt creeping in on me and several times that evening I was on the point of getting up, opening the door out to the hall, knocking on the living-room door and telling Thomas everything, maybe even suggesting that we went away together, but I never got any further than pondering whether to knock on the living-room door before walking in or not. I don't know why I felt I should knock first. Do monsters knock or do they just barge in? As if it were less terrifying to be visited by a polite monster.

288

I am sitting in the grey house on the rue de l'Ermitage and have just been reading an old gardening book that I found in a box of books in the loft. The chapter on kitchen gardens won't help me much in this kitchen, since you can't garden in the eighteenth of November and this house doesn't have a garden anyway. There are no rows of leeks or Swiss chard, there are no onions in boxes in the garden shed and there are no schemes for seed or crop rotation. I don't need to think about it being November or that my seasons are gone. I don't need to consider the fact that I am a guest because there's no one home in this house. There are no footsteps on the stairs or crossing the floors when I am sitting quietly at the kitchen table. I don't hear a hand or sleeve brushing a wall. I don't hear kettles on stoves. When I open the fridge the door closes softly again all by itself and the only gushing in the pipes is instigated by me.

I am alone. I am alone and I am safe. Safe from gushing and streaming, from rustling and crinkling, from fridge doors bumping against worktops, from coming and going, from clinking and crunching, from opening and closing and clattering. I am not safe from the rain. I can hear it on the roof and when it gets heavier I can see it on the kitchen window. It dissolves the scene outside the window, but that comes back. Same day, same weather, same rain. But I have got rid of the musty smell. I have removed some mildew from the wallpaper in the corners, I have cleaned the fridge, because there was a little bit of mould in there even though the door had been open, and I have washed the kitchen floor. When it gets cold in the house I switch on my fan heater and if that is not enough I turn the oven on. Or I bake bread or cook dishes that can sit and simmer quietly on the stove. So there is some sound after all.

298

I notice it most in the morning. Sometimes I feel as though I am waking to a completely different day. I think September. It's in the light from the window or a gust of wind when I open my door. A balmy breeze that is gone again seconds later. Fleeting glimpses, appearing and disappearing, as if

there were chinks in my day, as if there were another time running underneath my days, an ordinary year shining through
from below. I search for the chinks, I go into town and find
September, I sniff the air like a dog. It is there for a second
then gone again.

317

I have started making plans. I make plans in the woods. Not
in the courtyard at the back of the house at night. Not with
my telescope in the darkness. Not in the streets, as I roam
around with my umbrella and a bag over my shoulder, wondering whether I look like a monster or a person. But among
the trees, on woodland paths and in clearings covered in
leaves of yellow or brown. I went back for my winter boots
while Thomas was out. They were tucked away in a cupboard
in the hall, and now I go for walks in the woods. I don't follow Thomas's route and I don't run into him. My path almost
converges with his, but before I reach it I veer off in another
direction. I am not ready to meet him. I turn and go back the
way I came. The paths are soggy. I slip and slither about on
the leaves and where there are no leaves I can feel the damp
earth. It sucks at the soles of my winter boots, it clings to me,
and I have to pick up my feet up as I walk.

Thomas follows other paths. He follows paths covered in
stones or grit, but I am dressed for dirt tracks caked with
leaves, I steer clear of the river and the old watermill, I bear
towards the middle of the woods. It is November, but deep

145

in the woods there are still some leaves on the trees and I think September or possibly October. The woods seem to have opened up. There is something underneath my November day and the woods tug at me as if they wish me to stay. They cling to the soles of my boots, they want to tell me about September and October, but I keep walking, I know it is November.

I go out at different times of the day. It rains a little or the sun breaks through the trees. In the afternoon I walk around the edge of the woods, beside the fields. I make ready. I make plans on the paths and in the rain and after I have walked through the woods I go back to the house in the rue de l'Ermitage, sometimes I am wet with rain when I get back, sometimes I am just cold, but I carry my fan heater into the kitchen and shut the door, I turn on the heater, I boil water in my kettle, I switch on the oven, which has a grill at the top, and toast some bread under the glowing red element and before I know it the kitchen is warm and the day is over.

339

He came walking towards me. Thomas. He didn't see me until he was almost upon me. I was just a person sitting on a bench, but then I became Tara, right in front of him.

I had sat down on the bench next to the stone wall on the edge of the woods. There were a couple of cars in the car park some way off, but no people to be seen, not until Thomas came walking along the road. I saw him through the trees, walking, with no letters and parcels, only his bag over his shoulder.

He hadn't been expecting to meet me in the woods. He thought I was in Paris. He came towards me, I waved, he stopped short, taken aback.

So I told him everything. I asked him if he would like to sit down beside me on the bench. Or would he rather go for a walk through the woods? He would prefer to go for a walk through the woods, he said, and so we set off, walking side by side, while yet again I told him about the eighteenth of November, the whole story this time, with ghosts and monsters, with telescopes and estate agents and a grey house with a fridge that didn't bump against the corners of worktops but swung back and closed all by itself, with winter boots and mud that clung to your boots as you walked.

We stayed away from the wettest paths. We walked on grit and stones, we followed his route down to the old watermill by the river. We followed the paths along the banks and arrived back at the car park not long before the sky darkened. I insisted that he come with me. He was reluctant. I had told him about the house in the rue de l'Ermitage, but I had not told him about my plans.

I unlocked the door. He was my guest, even though the house was only on loan. I made coffee and served it in glasses because I only had one mug but there were plenty of glasses in the cupboard, so I poured coffee for us and we sat in the kitchen, listening to the rain. I had brought him indoors so he did not get caught in the rain. I had bought orange-flavoured chocolate, not in one of the usual supermarkets but in a small chocolate shop near the place Mignolet.

The plan, I said, was to go back to Paris. I wanted to close my circle. I wanted to get to the eighteenth of November when it came around again, one year on. I wanted him to come with me. I needed help. An anchor, a lifeline, a mooring. Someone who would hold fast. I had 339 days. I was coming up on a year. Was I sure? Yes, I was sure. Or almost sure. When I had accumulated 365 days a year would have passed because it wasn't a leap year, I said. I had checked.

I told him how I had been conscious of another time underneath my November days, a year with a September and an October. The world was porous, there were chinks in it, there was another year underneath. This thought had occurred to me before, but only now did I really feel it. Since moving into the house in the rue de l'Ermitage. I had become convinced of it during my walks in the woods. A new eighteenth of November was in the offing and that had to be the way out: to jump into the eighteenth of November when it came around again, to grab hold, to clamber on board a recognisable time. We could find the way together. We had to try to find the door leading out of the eighteenth of November.

We had to go back to where it all began. Would he come with me? He could be my anchor, my lifeline, my mooring. We could stay at the Hôtel du Lison as we usually did, we could get up and have breakfast at the hotel. We could witness the slice of bread hovering. Catch it before it fell, maybe. We could set the day to rights. We could return the books to their shelves. We could call on Philip and Marie, we could sit around the counter in the shop. The sestertius would be lying there in its transparent box. I was sure of it. The gas heater would be there in the back room, dust and all. Philip and Marie would be sitting at the counter. We could redress the balance of the day.

But Thomas demurred. How would we know what to do? There were lots of options, I said, we would find the right one. Together we would find a way out. I outlined various scenarios. We could reprise my first eighteenth of November together, we could end the day at the shop with Philip and Marie. We could fetch the gas heater from the back room, we could light it, I could burn my hand. We could repeat the whole thing, I said, but he wasn't sure, what good would it do to repeat a day which kept repeating itself anyway?

Or we could do the opposite, I said. Something else. A mirror image. A complete contrast. He could reprise my day. Maybe that was the answer. Maybe he was the missing piece. I could fill him in on all the details. That would be easy enough. It would entail a minor injury, but it would be quick. When it got warmer in the shop he would have to get up and give the gas heater a hefty push, placing his hand on the red-hot metal of the heater's top corner. It would be over in a second. He would hardly feel a thing. There were bowls and cold water in the shop. There would be plasters and antiseptic ointment for him. There would be ice cubes at the hotel. I would be there to help, he wasn't to worry.

I could see him looking around the kitchen, he shifted uneasily on his chair and shot a glance at the door into the hall. He was looking for a way out.

Or, I went on quickly, we could find other, completely different ways through the day. Whether it should be the one version or the other was something we could decide once we got there. But I was sure that we should wait till the year was up. Till the eighteenth of November came around again. I had felt the year sighing through the chinks in the eighteenth of November. I persisted: maybe if he checked how he felt he would feel October. Soon it would be November and when we were almost at the eighteenth we would set off.

He looked at me. I could tell he thought that I was mad, unreliable, mentally unstable. He ran an eye around the kitchen. He looked tired and suddenly I was aware of the musty smell that I thought I had got rid of. I looked at our empty glasses, at the rings of dark liquid that had formed in the bottoms of them and I felt how cold it was, even though I had switched on the fan heater when we came in.

150

Thomas felt that I should go back with him to our house. Apart from anything else he was hungry. I nudged the rest of the chocolate across the table, but he didn't touch it. We waited until the rain had abated then we switched off the heater and went out. On the way we passed a pizzeria and went in to buy a pizza for our dinner, and after a moment's indecision we decided to buy two different ones because we couldn't make up our minds.

I quickly calculated the effect it would have had on the world if this was how we had lived in the eighteenth of November ever since I had got back from Paris: 676 pizza boxes, 676 pizzas, but I said nothing and while I waited for our pizzas Thomas went to a wine shop a little further down the street and bought two bottles of wine, one white and one red, because he couldn't make up his mind.

I could tell by his face. He was bewildered. Maybe he was right: maybe I was mad. But he had confused cause and effect. I wasn't so mad as to imagine that I had lived through the eighteenth of November 339 times – I had been driven mad by living through the eighteenth of November 339 times. The eighteenth of November had rendered me peculiar. I wanted out. I wanted him to help me, but I already knew that this was a wish that would not be fulfilled. I could tell. He was caught in his own pattern and there was no help to be had from that quarter.

He would have preferred not to believe me, but that was not an option. As we were setting off into the woods I had been able to tell him that in a moment a car was going to drive into the car park behind us; I could tell when the sun would break through and predict the precise pattern of the rain. He had to believe me. But he was probably right in that I had become unreliable. I had lost my sense of judgement. I had not been able to maintain my common sense. This troubled him. He really just wanted to get the evening over with and wake up to a normal world. That was not an option either.

We spent the evening in our armchairs with pizza and red wine. He obviously didn't want to go to Paris. He didn't want to be part of my plans. He didn't think it would do any good. He felt we should wait, that I should stay at home with him. Until tomorrow, he said. He meant the nineteenth. But tomorrow will be the eighteenth, I said. He wasn't sure. He felt we ought to take one day at a time. There was always a chance, he said, that we would wake up to the nineteenth of November. Sooner or later time was surely bound to resume its progressive course, he said. All of a sudden maybe. To-morrow even. Maybe the fault in time would fix itself: we would go to bed, go to sleep and who knows, maybe we would wake up as T. & T. Selter in a house in Clairon-sous-Bois. On the nineteenth.

I had been hoping he would say this. But now it sounded all wrong. As if it was only something he was saying to avoid having to come with me, not because he was sitting in an armchair with a pizza and a feeling of hope that he wanted to share with me. Although perhaps that was too much to expect. Perhaps I shouldn't have suggested that he burn his hand. But I know that's not what did it. He would have said no anyway. I had just given him an excuse. A reason not to go. Extended a hand to him.

I insisted on making plans. He thought we should wait. You can't plan for everything, he said. Sometimes you just have to be ready. Take each day as it comes, be on the alert. Something will turn up. An opportunity. An escape route. Or maybe it would be better for me to go to Paris on my own, he said. My sharp eyes would show me the way. If I wandered about at the end of the year. With your gifts, he said. Your eye for detail.

He said this because he didn't want to go with me. He wanted to stay in his pattern. I knew it and he knew it and there was no reason to contradict him.

Thomas thought we should go to bed. That we should leave the possibilities of the night open. I didn't argue, but later that night, once he had gone to sleep, I tiptoed out of the bedroom. I went down the stairs and along the hall, slipped on my winter boots and laced them up. Took my coat from its hook, put it on and eased the door open. But just as I was on my way out I heard Thomas on the stairs. He said he knew where I was going. I nodded in the dark, closed the door behind me and walked back through the streets.

The night sky was almost completely overcast, but the clouds were beginning to break up and move away to the north-east as I walked back to my house in the rue de l'Ermitage. There was a light in the kitchen window because we had forgotten to switch it off when we left and the door was unlocked. The house was cold because we had remembered to turn off the heating. On the table were our glasses, which I cleared away, and the last of the chocolate, which I ate once I had fetched my papers and sat down at the table.

I still have my boots on but I have hung my coat over the back of the chair. I still have plans. Plans of a sort. Although I don't know if they can be called plans any more. They are loose and open-ended. What I have are scenarios and possibilities, not real plans. I imagine a way out of the eighteenth of November. I don't know what it looks like, this way, but I know that Thomas won't be coming with me.

340

An October day, I thought when I woke up. Late in the afternoon but rested. I was lying on the bed, fully dressed, my boots and coat the only things I had taken off. My boots lay flopped on the floor, light fell through the window for a moment before a cloud covered the sun. A moment later the cloud had passed and sunlight filled the room. I rose, picked up my boots and took them downstairs with me. I left them in the hall and opened the door onto the courtyard, where the sun shone down on the flagstones from a patch of blue October sky, but shortly afterwards, when it began to feel like November again, I came back inside, shut the door and sat down at the table. My papers lie in front of me, my coat still hangs over the back of a chair; it's chilly in here, but I've switched on my fan heater and I have calculated that it must be the twenty-third of October. That must be what I can feel. The sunshine is October sun, even if only in glimpses.

348

I am growing uneasy. I count the days and I have written # 348 in my notebook. I count November days but if I check I can detect a last glimmer of October.

I am preparing to leave this place. I pack my things. Yesterday, while Thomas was out, I carried the last bits and pieces back to our house: a couple of books, some kitchen utensils, a shoe brush and a tin of shoe polish I had borrowed. My winter boots are back in the cupboard where I found them. I have taken some paper from the shelf in the guest room and put it in my bag along with pencils and a pen. As if there were something to tell.

I had cleared up the last things in the guest room and was about to leave the house when I remembered that I would need my phone. I searched the room and eventually found it. It had fallen on the floor and was lying in the dust and fluff under the bed. It was totally dead, of course, but I popped it into my bag, went out, locked the door and slipped the key into the front pocket of my bag.

It felt like a farewell. I had been a guest, and the key in my bag had been on loan. I ought to have handed it in, but instead I walked into town to have my phone checked. It turned out that there was a problem with a SIM card or a memory card or something and the phone itself needed charging, but it was soon up and running again. I bought a new charger because I don't know what has happened to the old one and now I think I am ready to leave. I have packed my passport, got out clothes, gathered together my little stack of books from the seventeenth and eighteenth of November and set them on the table. I have put all my papers in the black cardboard folder and I have my notebook containing the strokes and numbers marking the days. The whole lot is now lying beside me in the kitchen in the rue de l'Ermitage and I am preparing to set off. I want to get out of the eighteenth of November. I wish to find a way and the thought makes me uneasy.

349

I can feel it now: a year running under my eighteenths of November. I cannot think of it any other way. I am closing a circle. I am on my way out of my November year. I am moving into another year. Another time.

This morning I left the house in the rue de l'Ermitage, locked the door and left the key under a plant pot in the courtyard.

I walked to the station, boarded a train to Lille and travelled from there to Paris, and now I am sitting in my room in the Hôtel du Lison. It is the afternoon. It is the same city, the same room and yet it is something else. It is a year nearing its end. That is where I am going, to an end full of chinks and cracks. I am on my way.

When I walked through the door of the Hôtel du Lison the receptionist looked up from her computer screen and reached for the key to Room 16 as if nothing had happened. I took the key and went up the stairs to the hotel room that I left almost a year ago. The bed had been made and a few of my belongings lay on the bedspread: a small box of mints and a dark-green pen with the logo '7ème Salon Lumières', which I had brought back from the auction on the seventeenth of November and must have forgotten.

There was nothing home-like about the room. Familiar, yes, but not home-like. I don't know if I have a home. My home is no longer the house in Clairon, where Thomas follows his pattern, where he has probably hung up his wet coat in the hall and is going up and down stairs and across floors. My home is not the room overlooking the apple tree and a wood-pile. My home is not the grey house in the rue de l'Ermitage. I don't belong. I live in the eighteenth of November. I have moved into a November day, but now I want out. I don't want to stay here any more. I am preparing to leap out of the eighteenth of November.

I am sitting at the table in my room. I am chewing mint pastilles from the seventeenth of November. From a time when the days followed one another. Sixteenth, seventeenth, eighteenth. Nineteenth.

I am trying to tie up time, to get to the nineteenth. I write with a green pen and think of the nineteenth of November: come closer, nineteenth, step inside.

350

Late yesterday afternoon I walked past Philip Maurel's shop. The lights were on and I could see that Marie was alone. I walked up and down the pavement on the other side of the street a couple of times before cutting across the road, stopping in front of the window and peering down into the shop. On the counter lay three coins, each displayed in its own transparent box. The time was twenty past four. I didn't know exactly when Philip would be back, only that it would be before five. I wavered for a moment, but then I descended the few steps to the shop, opened the door and stepped inside. Marie came towards me from the other end of the shop showing no sign of recognition. I said hello and asked to see the coins on display. She showed them to me and kindly told me something about each one. She immediately sensed that the coin in the middle was the one that interested me most and informed me that it was a Roman sestertius portraying the Emperor Antoninus Pius. I nodded, picked up the box and beheld a coin very like the one I had given Thomas. Or rather: it was the same coin.

There's no point in pretending that I am in any doubt. It was my sestertius and it had returned to its place on the counter. Next to the sestertius on the one side was a silver coin bearing the images of Castor and Pollux and on the other a copper denar showing the Lighthouse of Alexandria. They were the same coins that had been set out on the counter on my first eighteenth of November and there was no doubt in my mind that the sesterius was the coin that I had purchased.

I wavered. I briefly considered trying to gain access to the back room, to inspect the dust on the blue gas cylinder, but I didn't have much time and I suddenly had the feeling that I ought to tread very carefully in the eighteenth of November if I was to have any hope of escaping from it. I was afraid of setting the day in motion and so, rather too abruptly and perhaps a little rudely, I thanked Marie and hurried out of the shop. I ran up the steps, crossed the road and went into a small grocery shop, where I picked up a basket and ducked into an aisle just before Philip came walking along the street. He stopped at the window of his shop, waved to Marie and went down the steps.

A minute later, when I left the grocery shop, the time was quarter to five. I glanced around then walked briskly away, hugging the wall, cut back across the road and carried on down the rue Almageste. This was clearly the same eighteenth of November as the last time I had been here. Outside a shop further down the street I saw a dark-brown dog waiting for its owner. I was certain that I had seen the owner come out of a shop and collect her dog shortly before I arrived at Philip's shop on my first eighteenth of November and sure enough: moments later the owner came out of the shop carrying a distinctive turquoise carrier bag and untied the dog's leash from a railing near the shop door.

Darkness was falling on the streets around the rue Almageste. I followed the rue Renart to the small square at the end of the street and after emerging from the passage du Cirque I crossed the boulevard Chaminade and sat down at a café just around the corner, in the rue Rainette.

These are streets I have known for years. From my life before Thomas, because I lived here for a year when I was a student. It wasn't until a couple of years later that I met Thomas, and later Philip, through mutual friends who lived in a flat in the passage du Cirque. They moved away from there long ago, but the streets and parks I know so well are still here, Philip's shop is here, the Hôtel Lison is here, as are shops I used to frequent and our colleagues in the antiquarian bookshops. These are haunts I have often revisited, alone or with Thomas, but now it is a well-known world in a time that has ground to a halt. I long for a world where time passes. A world where the eighteenth of November is a day like any other, a day you can put behind you.

A little later, when I left the café and was making my way back to the hotel I came by an antiquarian bookshop I had never visited. The light from the window fell on the rack of books outside on the pavement. Some greyish plastic sheeting had been folded back from the books, ready for laying over them if it should rain. But that wouldn't be necessary. I could have told the people in the shop that they could happily take their plastic sheeting in again, because it wouldn't rain until late that night, by which time the shop would long since have closed with the books safe inside.

I stopped for a moment, but I didn't go in. Instead I walked back to my hotel, where I went to bed and where I have now woken yet again to the same eighteenth of November. I have had breakfast, I have sat with the usual newspaper and I have seen a slice of bread fall, seen the discreet retrieval, a croissant on a plate, and it is all far too familiar.

354

How am I to get out of the eighteenth of November? How did I get into it? Did I enter through the wrong door? The door of repetitions? I don't know. I look for exits. I mean, if you can get in you must be able to get out. I think to myself. How do you open a door that won't open? Do you kick it in? Break it down? Set fire to it? Locksmith? Wishful thinking? Secret codes? Magic words? I can't help feeling there's something I ought to do. That something can be changed. That I have to correct a mistake. That I have to find the right moment, then act.

But I'm not sure any more. I walk through the streets and the eighteenth of November suddenly seems very fragile, full of doors that could all too easily be kicked in. I wander around the china shop of the eighteenth of November. China. Glass. Crystal. From floor to ceiling. I can move through the day like a bull, like a butterfly. What should I do? Should I barge my way out of my day or should I flit and flutter lightly around the world? Am I a butterfly, which can cause a hurricane by flapping its wings? A bull charging at walls to break them down? I don't know. I roam my streets, thinking that it is easy to do something. To act is easy. To break down doors. But what if you don't have to break down doors? What if you have to knock very softly on a door? But which door?

355

There must be a difference to grab hold of. There must be a variation. A change. But what does a difference look like? I don't know. But if I know my day, if I know my streets, it must be possible for me to see if something new occurs.

I no longer feel there's something I ought to do to the eighteenth of November, that I have to piece together a jigsaw puzzle, turn a handle, perform some action. I don't have the idea that I need to break into the day's happenings or move the objects of the eighteenth of November around.

I have the feeling there's something I should see, that something new will break through when the year is up. That hairline cracks have already appeared. I envisage a change in those well-known streets, that in all repetitions there is a variation, a difference.

But what constitutes a difference? Is it a sound? A smell? Is it a colour or a shape? Is it green or blue? How small is my difference? Is it an incident, an action? Will something unexpected suddenly happen? Something notable or extraordinary? Will it be something perfectly normal and quite commonplace? Or will it be something that doesn't happen? Something missing? A disappearance?

I envisage a new eighteenth of November, but I don't know how it will differ from the old one. I have the feeling that the weather will be different. But will it be warmer or colder? Will there be an unexpected shower of rain? I envisage a break, a change. But how will this change come about? Will it happen when I least expect it, or will it call for alertness, concentration? Will I have to listen for it, will I have to smell or feel or see? I don't know. I look for details. I am watchful and ready.

I wait, prepare myself for when the moment comes, and until then: patience, patience, patience.

356

It's hard to be patient when you don't know what you're waiting for. It's hard to spot a difference in the host of incidents in the day.

Wherever I go things are the same. There are the same shops with the same customers. The same overflowing litter bins at the entrance to the park near the rue Renart, where three burger bags and a red-lettered pizza box have fallen out of the bin and settled under a bench. There are the same cheeses in the cheese shop a little further along the street, where two signs twirl around on their cheeses like ballet dancers caught mid-pirouette on their respective stages. There is a green door covered in graffiti in an odd pale-blue colour where a woman stands with a foot in the doorway, her eyes scanning the street and another woman with shopping bags in both hands is trying to indicate that she's coming: she raises one hand, but the bag in it is too heavy so she merely waggles it about a bit.

There are people wearing coats and shoes. There is a man crossing the street, a phone being pulled out. There are doors being opened and lights being switched off. There is a woman who has dropped her loose change all over the pavement, the coins dance around her for a moment then come to rest and she picks them up, one at a time. I am standing on the other side of the street, she was there yesterday and she is there today. But what is it that's different, if she is my difference? Is it the look in her eyes, or the number of coins spilling onto the street, are there now seven instead of five? How will I tell the difference? Is it the streetlights, coming on at a different time? How will I be able to tell? Will it be five minutes earlier or two minutes later?

I need to know my ground if I am to see when the light changes. I roam my streets. I am watchful, I read the incidents on the streets and store them in my memory.

361

I feel at home in the hustle and bustle of the streets. I know my streets. I have looked up at the windows of the buildings, I have looked down at the pavement, I have read newspapers in cafés and watched people entering and leaving, and every day it is the same people and the same newspapers. I have walked past Maurel Numismatique. I have seen Marie setting out a sign on the street at opening time and I have seen Philip turning off the lights in the shop. I have seen him lock the door and I have followed him to a café where he meets Marie at quarter past eight. I have watched them from a distance. I won't disturb them. I won't disturb their day.

I have heard ambulances and cars and a bicycle bell that made two pedestrians jump with fright. I have walked along gravel paths in the little park near the rue Renart, on morning pavements wet with rain and down the dry streets of the afternoon. I have heard bottle banks being emptied in the morning and vans reversing down narrow alleyways. I have seen a truck stop to deliver office chairs and two men dragging them across the pavement and into a building, chair after chair, two at a time, sometimes three, all black, on castors and covered in plastic, forty-seven in all. I counted.

362

This is a world I know and I am ready. To leap. To grab hold of a sudden change. Or ready to dive, I think. Why does it have to be a leap? Maybe I should be getting ready to hold my breath.

I am in two minds. I sit in Room 16, thinking that I don't know whether to leap or dive. One moment I am treading carefully through the day, poised to leap, and the next I am taking a deep breath, getting ready to dive.

365

I woke before it was light. The streets were still wet when I went out into the morning gloom. It was a little after five o'clock when I left the hotel and it had just stopped raining.

I am on high alert from the moment I wake. My consciousness kicks in, my senses are on overload, my nervous system is buzzing. I know I'm not there yet, not quite. Everything seems like a day I know, but I can't help looking for sudden changes.

If time were passing this would be the seventeenth of November, the day before the eighteenth. Tomorrow it will be the eighteenth of November again, because a year has passed. Or has it? Have I counted correctly? I go over all my calculations. No, it isn't a leap year. I have taken my notebook out of my bag. I have counted my strokes and my days and the result is always the same: this is the last day of my year and tomorrow is the eighteenth of November.

I am ready. I look for signs that this is a different day but all I find are repetitions so I will have to wait till tomorrow. Nonetheless, I am on the alert. Tense and watchful. Poised. I am on the lookout for a change that I can grab hold of, a difference, a shift. It is evening. I sit in Room 16. Maybe I will wake to a difference. If I sleep.

366

I dreamed I was swimming and when I woke I told myself that all would become clear. I could float around in my day, all I had to do was swim. Or drift, I thought, like that drifting slice of bread, hovering in mid-air before it fell.

I had breakfast. Drifting. Swimming. Got up, fetched some food from the buffet and sat down again. Breathed. Lowered my shoulders. I was in water, it felt light and I glided smoothly around. Or it was air and I was drifting gently, like a very light slice of bread, into my day.

Whatever happened, I thought to myself, I would know when it happened. When the time came. I would have to drift around, tread water. I went out into my day. The same day, but it felt benign. Open, full of possibility and replete with detail and incident and movements that could change direction at any moment.

I had one day to go and I went with it. There was no plan. There was an outline, one which I could follow, floating, gently.

There was no goal, no prey to be caught. I was not a circling raptor, a vulture, a shark, a big cat poised to spring. I was not on my guard. This was something else. I was on a journey. On my way home, I thought. I was travelling on an open ticket, with no itinerary. I journeyed through the minutiae of the streets, in a universe replete with minor incidents, a host of objects and occurrences and sensations all crowded together in my memory.

So many things, colours. So many signs, shops, people, so many articles in the shops, so many handles on so many doors, so many shoes walking along the streets, so many coats, so much stitching in so many shoes, in so many garments, so many stones on the kerbs of so many pavements, so many details, a maelstrom of objects, of tiny details on these objects, all of these things I had amassed from the streets of the eighteenth of November, layer upon layer, so many that my mind had to cram them together, but I glided through it all with unaccustomed ease and found myself thinking how strange it was that one could float so lightly through such a compact world.

Somewhere in this mass of details there had to be a difference, I thought. Something to grab hold of. If there was another eighteenth of November under my day it would trickle through the cracks. I would see differences, I would close in, grab hold, climb aboard, float along.

I went around places I knew. Places I had visited on my first eighteenth of November and then again and again. I came by the two antiquarian bookshops where I had collected the copies of *Histoire des Eaux Potables* and *The Heavenly Bodies*, but I only stopped for a moment outside their windows. I passed Philip's shop. Marie was there as usual. I saw her from the street and walked on. I moved with this ease through a day that seemed the same, but I was ready, the day would open up and I would leave it by the same sluices that had drawn me in. The same currents. Ocean currents, air currents. I swam, I drifted. I waited.

Until, all of a sudden, a voice called out to me. Loudly. Called my name. Tara. And then again. Louder still.

I turned in the direction of the voice. It was me he meant. Philip. I turned around and he came towards me. Smiling.

He was delighted to see me. He had had no idea I was in town. Was Thomas with me? And had I time to come back to the shop with him? He was going there now. He had actually had a couple of errands to run, but they could wait. There was someone he would like me to meet, he said. His girlfriend, Marie. It was ages since he had spoken to me. How was Thomas? They would come to Clairon-sous-Bois soon, he and Marie. They had been talking about it only the other day, in fact. So much had happened, he said as I fell into step with him. Confused, because this was not a possibility I had considered. Meeting Philip on the street was not one of my scenarios.

I had not checked what he did in the afternoon before we met at the shop and it had never occurred to me to do so.

He had just come from the bank, he said. He had had a meeting there. He and Marie wanted to buy the flat on the third floor above his shop. The old lady who had owned it had died a couple of months earlier and her heirs wanted to sell it. The flat was not in particularly good condition, or rather: it was chock-full of stuff. The owner had been a collector. Not in the normal sense of the word, though. A collector in the extreme. A hoarder.

We had reached the shop and as we were going down the steps I saw Marie standing at the counter, arranging some coins on a display tray.

Philip introduced me to Marie and said that now they had two pieces of good news: I had come to see them and the bank had given them the green light to buy the flat. Marie and I chatted about this and that, about Thomas and Clairon-sous-Bois, while Philip nipped out again to buy a bottle of wine. Better make it bubbly, Marie said as she slid her tray back into a display cabinet in the adjoining room, because we have something to celebrate.

Philip returned with a bottle of champagne and put it in the fridge, and while he was locking the shop door and hanging a sign in the window Marie and I went through the back room to the back stairs and out into the dim stairwell. We had trouble finding the light switch out there, but Philip was right behind us. He had Marie's coat with him, not wanting her to get cold, and as he handed it to her I managed to locate the switch and turn on the light. We climbed the stairs to the door on the third floor, a big brown door which Philip unlocked for us with a key he had in his pocket. The old lady's heirs had lent him the key. They were keen to sell as quickly as possible and preferably for Philip and Marie to take over the flat as it was: bearing the clear marks of years of neglect and full of stuff that would have to be removed before the place could be done up.

All over the flat there were boxes and heaps of stuff: piles of newspapers, mounds of clothing and bookshelves packed with books and magazines. In the largest room in the flat, which must at one time have been a sitting room, tall stacks of newspapers covered the floor, with only a narrow passageway snaking between them. We followed the path between the stacks to the next room, where the walls were lined with boxes, and clothes, loads of clothes and, at the very back, a full cat litter tray. The cat was no more, Philip said. Or cats. There had been two.

This was where they were going to live. Philip and Marie. There was plenty to do, but they could start almost immediately. Tomorrow even, Philip said. As soon as they had signed the contract.

I followed them along the endless, twisting path between the mountains of rubbish. I wanted to get out of the eighteenth of November and there was nothing for it but to follow along. I remember feeling rather confused. It felt strange, I thought, almost as if I had found my difference, my change. Maybe I had already jumped to another day, to a new universe, on my way to the nineteenth. With stacks of newspapers, with mounds of clothes and a cat litter tray at the end of a winding road.

We worked our way back along the narrow path through the rooms, back to the hall and a smaller room which had been more or less cleared. This was where the resident of the flat had slept with her cats and her most treasured possessions. Her heirs had removed everything that wasn't to be thrown away. They were hoping that the new owners would see to the rest. It was a daunting prospect, Marie said, but not impossible. It would take a while, though, there was so much to be done. The owner of the flat had lived there all her days. A whole life compressed into one flat. A time capsule, Marie said. Nothing had been done to the place for years, the kitchen was over a hundred years old, the bathroom was tiny and probably just as old. They had a lot of plans for the place, but before anything else it would have to be cleared out.

We left the flat and Philip locked the door. A dark and surprisingly heavy door with a large knocker in the middle of it, a brass bird as far as I could make out, although it was so black with tarnish it was hard to tell, and beneath it was an indecipherable and almost obliterated name, something beginning with G.

After locking up Philip tried the door knocker, rapping the door lightly with the beak of the bird or whatever it was, and asked if anyone was home. Marie smiled. Not yet, she said. Anything and everything, yes. Anyone, no.

Back downstairs in the shop Marie opened the bottle of champagne and fetched some water glasses which she filled to the brim, then we drank to their new home, to my visit and to love. And once we had toasted Marie refilled our glasses and they asked me about my trip. What was I doing in town, how long had I been here, how long was I staying? Would I have time to meet up with them again – later that evening perhaps, or the day after? What were my plans? Marie had to pop out, she had a few things to do, but she wouldn't be long.

I hesitated. My day had taken an unexpected turn. I had been walking around at the end of a year full of eighteenths of November, I had roamed the streets with my senses sharpened and all my systems on high alert, ready to spring into another time, and now here I was, standing at the counter in Philip's shop, drinking toasts and having to say what plans I had for the day.

I had no plans, I said, not any longer, and then suddenly it all came out, I told them everything: about my deadlocked day, that I had paid them a visit. I told them what had happened, how we had eaten together around the shop counter almost exactly a year ago, or the number of days that would have made up a year, that Marie and I had dragged the dust-covered heater through from the back-shop. They hadn't told me about the flat, but we had chatted about lots of other things.

For some reason I had expected to be believed. I hadn't anticipated any doubt. I mean, why would anyone make up a story like that? But I was wrong. Perhaps Philip didn't need anyone bringing an element of disquiet into his new life with Marie. They didn't need oddities. Philip could see his future with Marie. He did not want deadlocked days, he did not want disquiet.

It was when I told them about my accident with their heater that I saw the disquiet in their faces, that and something else which I had not expected to see. A vacillation between credulity and doubt, an uncertainty which sprang not from unease at the thought of the fault in time I had told them about, but more likely from a growing scepticism, denial, a weighing up of my credibility perhaps.

It was, though, when I showed Philip the very faint scar left by my burn and then led him through to the dusty heater in the back room that he seemed to make up his mind. That it wasn't true. That I was on my way out of the door again. That he had his doubts about my story.

When I told them about meeting Marie in the shop on my second eighteenth of November and how I had bought a sestertius which had then returned to the shop and was now lying in its box on the counter, the mood changed and just as I finished telling them about purchasing the coin Philip reached for the box and, with a quick glance at Marie, popped the sestertius, box and all, into a little carrier bag and handed it to me. As if he could put things right by pretending to believe me. Or be rid of the whole business if I took the sestertius away with me.

I took the bag from him. And it was as if we suddenly became aware that something was wrong. That we were standing in the shop, drinking champagne, that we still had our coats on, but no one made any move to take them off or to sit down. None of us knew what to say or do. We had no explanations or answers and the next minute I was out the door, bag in hand.

Philip had mumbled something about how we must get together. Tomorrow, he said. But I was to keep the sestertius.

Out on the street I was struck by a sense of unreality. For a second I was still sure that this was another day, the nineteenth or a new version of the eighteenth, because it felt as though something had shifted, and I walked off down the rue Almageste with a faint hope of change, but with every step I took I became more and more convinced that this was exactly the same day as before.

I wondered why Philip hadn't told me about them buying the flat the first time we had spoken. But I could find no explanation. I wanted to believe that it was because I now inhabited an entirely different version of the eighteenth of November, but I was already sure that everything was the same as before. The weather was the same as on the other eighteenths of November; a little further down the street I saw a woman tying up a dark-brown dog outside a shop and after a few minutes during which I tried to act as though I was interested in the window display of the shop next door she came out again carrying a turquoise carrier bag, untied the leash and walked away with the dog.

The light was starting to fade and minutes later the street lamps came on as usual. I walked along with my bag over my shoulder and the little carrier bag containing the sestertius in my hand and nothing had happened. Everything looked the same, but there seemed to be fewer details. There were only streets and shops and cafés and people. I walked with ordinary steps along ordinary streets. I did not float through a replete universe, I did not swim through an ocean of minute detail and I had no idea where I was going.

I had ruined my chance of visiting Philip and Marie. I couldn't go back to the shop. It was not a plan that had failed because there had been no plan, but I couldn't go back and start my evening again. I couldn't sit at the old desk that served as a counter and talk about the big demand for illustrated works from the eighteenth century, about the auction and my latest finds. I couldn't tell them about love or about the apple tree in our garden, about leeks and Swiss chard. We couldn't sit there chatting about life on the rue Almageste, about that autumn's political unrest, about a hunger for history and the growing demand for Roman coins. It was too late. My evening stood wide open, anything could happen, I thought to myself, but nothing happened. It was as if there was a hole in my congested universe and the details were trickling out, so all that was left of my world was the outline. Simple incidents. Ordinary objects.

I spent the evening in a café I had been to a couple of times before. There weren't many customers and I sat down at a table by the window with a cup of coffee and the sestertius in its bag on the table in front of me. Later, as the other tables began to fill up with diners and I could see that I was taking up too much space at my table for four, I moved to a small table at the back. I ordered a single glass of wine and sat for a while browsing through a newspaper, but I had read it before, it was full of all-too-familiar events, and by this time the back of the café was also beginning to fill up with people and plates and glasses and cutlery so eventually I decamped to the street and wandered around for a while before turning and going back to the hotel.

Out in the chill air I could breathe more easily and I strolled steadily through the night. The bag containing the sestertius rustled slightly and I could hear my footsteps on the pavement, but otherwise all I could hear was the city traffic, a backdrop of sound. It felt empty, but with the emptiness came a sense of relief: a well-known evening, an outline without too many details. There was something refreshing about the lack of detail, the lack of imaginings and scenarios and alertness and condensation.

When I got back to the hotel I put the little bag with the sestertius on the table in my room. I didn't unpack it, but a little later, after I had undressed and got into bed, I laid it next to me on the cover, bag and all.

I am sitting up in bed with my papers in front of me and it feels as though there is a hole in my eighteenth of November. As though there is a way out, but it is no longer one of the ways out that I had imagined. I don't know what is happening. There's nothing to do but wait and see what the night will bring.

The eighteenth of November is almost over. A year has passed and I am ready to make room for the nineteenth.

I leave the day open. I go with the day. I flow with it wherever it may go. I let myself be carried along by the current.
Now I swim. Dive.

On the Calculation of Volume II

The second volume of the landmark European masterpiece

I was sure that through careful listening you could solve any problem that might arise. If you really listened. The great questions in life. Everything.

A year has passed, but Tara still wakes up to the same newspapers and the same blank faces when she explains that she has seen this all before. Until, one morning, she boards a train and finds herself in a new day. It is still the eighteenth of November, but the faces are different, the weather is colder.

She realises that she has found a way out of her endless autumn. By moving across Europe rather than through time, she can collect the ingredients for the seasons: the thin film of ice on puddles, the fresh spring breeze, the blazing summer sun. As she travels, she begins to hope for a new future, one that will run in parallel to the eighteenth of November, one that she must build for herself.

'What the best novels can do is open up spaces. And she has opened a space in time, and it is absolutely, absolutely incredible.' Karl Ove Knausgård

'A total explosion: Solvej Balle has blown through to a new dimension of literary exploration.' Nicole Krauss

'Solvej Balle is a prodigious writer who, miraculously, finds the subtlest, most fascinating differences in repetition.' Hernan Díaz

faber